# Lake People

# Lake People

A NOVEL

# ABI MAXWELL

ALFRED A. KNOPF · NEW YORK · 2013

5043 4405 2/13

THIS IS A BORZOI BOOK
PUBLISHED BY ALFRED A. KNOPF

Copyright © 2013 by Abi Maxwell

All rights reserved. Published in the United States
by Alfred A. Knopf, a division of Random House, Inc., New York,
and in Canada by Random House of Canada Limited, Toronto.

www.aaknopf.com

Knopf, Borzoi Books, and the colophon are registered trademarks
of Random House, Inc.

Library of Congress Cataloging-in-Publication Data

Maxwell, Abi.
Lake people : a novel / Abi Maxwell. — 1st ed.
p.   cm.
"This is a Borzoi book."
ISBN 978-0-307-96165-5
I. Title.
PS3613.A898L35 2012
813'.6—dc23                    2012013948

Jacket photograph © by Lauren Burke/Iconica/Getty Images
Jacket design by Kelly Blair

Manufactured in the United States of America

First Edition

*This book is dedicated to my grandmother*

*Eleanor Pearson Keller.*

# Lake People

# 1982

IN THE COLD and windy days after I was born, I was deposited into an old canoe on the big lake. I have recently discovered this. I like to think my birth parents believed that this lake would hold me, keep me safe, but I don't see how that could possibly be true, for it turns out I come from a long line of people swallowed by these waters. My name is Alice, and by the time I was born, unwanted, the belief that there were places in the lake where the floor of the world either dropped out or was never put in had settled itself deep into my blood.

But the canoe wasn't floating freely. It was tied up in the boathouse where it would be found, just east of the Kettleborough Pier. Even in the days before I knew the story of my birth, I would stand on that pier in the evening, when the sky and the lake become indecipherable from each other, and look out three miles across the water to Bear Island, that fated place that I now know drew my ancestors in. In that light, it looks as though the island just floats, not within this life and not without it, but unattached, and free.

Eleonora was the first in our line to settle out on that island. She would be my great-great-grandmother. I always knew of her—if you live in our town you know her story—but I never did know I had some special connection to her. She came alone from Sweden as a teenager, and by the time she arrived she had faced some terrible trouble, and by the end of her life her trouble had not stopped. Because of this, people in Kettleborough like to believe she committed some significant amount of wrong.

The lake was frozen when Eleonora and her four children crossed from mainland to the island. Her husband had just died. On cold, gray days I can imagine her family walking across the ice in a single-file line, their suitcases in hand. They would have worn long wool coats, and the youngest child's would have been a hand-me-down, and still too long for him, so as he walked at the back of the line the fabric would have brushed upon the thin layer of snow, marking a temporary trail of the family's journey to their end.

In all, there were between twenty and thirty families who settled out on that island. All of them were Swedes, and all of them had taken the four-hour train ride from Boston to our pier and then crossed over. Eleonora's first winter out on Bear was a truly frozen one, so cold she felt she could grab handfuls of air and put them in her pocket. Despite this she began to build a cabin, which is what the newly arrived always did. However, my great-great-grandmother differed from the others in that she was a single woman and she neither asked for nor accepted help from anyone. While she worked she and her family stayed with the man who had first settled the island, sleeping in a row on his floor. It took only one week. When she brought her children to see the cabin, they were shocked to find that in their short time on Bear Island their mother not only had built a sturdy home for them, but had hunted and carved deer meat and hung the skins to dry; had cut and stacked enough wood to last through winter; had brought a woodstove from mainland; had built beds for them all; and had stocked the kitchen with flour, sugar, oats, salt, coffee, and everything else they might need. Such skills of survival were all new to Eleonora. They had risen up in her suddenly, as though straight from the island itself, and their arrival filled the children with what I can only see as a cruel sense of security.

But for some reason the lake gave them ten good years. Maybe that time was intended to earn their trust, or to build Eleonora's strength. Perhaps in the tenth year their family committed some offense against the water. More likely, there is no sense to be made of why, that year, their family's luck ended as a dark, cold winter streaked across the lake with a wind so sharp it bit at their naked cheeks. Most of the islanders wanted to pack up and head for mainland, for comfort and safety. Not Eleonora.


One morning that winter Eleonora's elder daughter, Ida, said she had to go to shore. She left her husband and infant daughter—my grandmother Sophie—and she went to be swallowed by the lake. The story told in Kettleborough is that on that morning Ida was drawn out upon the frozen water by the most beautiful of calls. The ice was as thick as an old maple, yet Ida had scarcely walked twenty steps upon it when the lake opened its mouth. First her feet dropped under, and then her hips came forward in one slow, consenting wave. Her arms swept upward and then, without sound, Ida dropped into the winter of the lake.

There is no question about the exact spot where this took place, for immediately after she dropped below, one pointed black rock rose up from the depths, and continued rising until it stood as high as Ida had. After that, other pointed rocks rose in its wake. Today a forest of these black rocks stands out there, marking the place where my ancestors first discovered that our lake is boundless as the sky.

The rocks are shaped as witch hats, so naturally the people of the island named them the Witches, and they knew to stay away. But on that first night after Ida vanished a bear appeared on the shore nearest to those rocks. It had been killed, its heart removed in one clean slice. Eleonora believed it to be a sign—of what, we never knew—and wanted the bear put in the place where her daughter had vanished. The people agreed. They found an old plank of wood and rolled the bear atop it, and then they pushed the vessel toward that tallest rock. It soared forward as though pulled by some invisible cord, yet when it stopped at the base of the rock, where the ice was now so thin that water bubbled upward, it did not sink. That was on the longest, darkest night of the year. A group of men kept watch through the night. They were waiting for the bear to be taken in, but they must have also been waiting for Ida to rise once more. Neither happened until spring, when the bear finally dropped below without witness. By then the people had come to say that though the site of the Witches was a place to be swallowed, it was also a place where a being might float. Still, they knew to take no risks. Their sharp warnings passed down through the generations, and until this year, so far as anyone knows, no one and no thing had ventured into that forest of rocks since the days of those lake people.

.    .    .

Sometimes I try to think of Eleonora's life before the island, to see her as a woman who presses her clothes and attends church, who bargains sensibly in her broken English with the vegetable man down at the market. Yet the Eleonora who remains in my mind is one whose skin has turned to leather. She dresses in the hides and furs of bear and deer, she eats raw fish, and she howls alone at night. But this can't possibly be the woman she was, either. At least not before she was left alone on the island.

After Ida vanished, Eleonora was left with one daughter, two sons, a widowed son-in-law, a granddaughter, and a fear of the living lake. When the ice melted, she began to drop offerings into the water—a serving of meat, an apple they had gotten on mainland. She sent prayers into the water, too, and the stories in town say that those prayers begged for forgiveness, though for what it was never said. Anyway, it did no good. The following winter, on a seamless blue day, her two sons and her son-in-law crossed the ice with a sled full of deer meat to trade for a good, sturdy new window for Eleonora's cabin. By now they had learned that the ice was not to be trusted, so at their side they towed a canoe, which they could jump into if the ice should break. But on the walk back to the island, only Eleonora's sons held on to the canoe, for their brother-in-law carried the window. They crossed in front of the Witches just as a great wind swept forward. Instinctively the boys jumped into that boat. When they looked back, they saw that rather than turning from the Witches, Ida's widower was headed straight for them, saying he heard the most beautiful of calls. The boys watched as the mouth of the lake split open at the rocks and traveled toward them. Their brother-in-law held that window high in front of his body and he looked through it, straight at the boys, as he dropped below.

When the boys turned back to face toward home they realized that they, too, had fallen into the open path of water. They unfastened the paddles from the sides of their boat and tried to push their way back onto the ice, but they could not do it. Finally, when they had expended all of their energy, that call came into them, too. They paddled up the path toward its source, straight to the center of the Witches. Here they let go of their paddles. Their boat began to slowly spin. With each turn it sank a little deeper, until finally the boat and its boys were underwater. They reached out to grasp each other, and there today those boys remain, their arms stretched above their heads and their hands braided into each other's, their bodies spinning slowly, as a net.

Winter was harsh, the Witches were cruel, and the people no longer trusted the lake. They decided to pack their belongings and return to the lives they had left behind. Eleonora's one remaining child, Signe, packed their family's belongings. Yet when she took her mother's arm to lead her to shore, Eleonora would not go. Instead she placed a kiss upon the head of her granddaughter, and she told Signe to go to Kettleborough and raise Ida's baby as her own.

Signe followed her mother's instructions. What else was she to do? Perhaps she protested, but she must have known she would be no match for her fierce mother. She left, and my great-great-grandmother went wild on that wild island. She took to killing bear with a jackknife, slicing into their fur and pulling forth their hearts. She kept a lantern lit on each end of the island, a beacon for travelers, and when they stopped for rest she offered a roof and a bed in trade for liquor, wool, and grains. And, for the rest of her days, Eleonora dropped offerings into the lake that had stolen her family. She dropped an ax and a bottle of whiskey, a pair of shoes, an old silver ring, the heart of a bear.

Meanwhile, on shore, people told stories of the beautiful call that had drawn Eleonora's family into the lake. I used to imagine it in the way so many in Kettleborough do, as the clear call of one of our lake's loons.

But now I have heard the call, and I know that is not accurate. It does indeed sound like a loon, but the sound is apart from all else, carried across the water and delivered to the listener in the softest of hands. As it travels it splits the air open, so that only that call remains—stark and final and brilliant—and its listener can do nothing but float toward it.

# PART ONE

# My Heavenly Days

## 1910–1962

MY AUNT SIGNE kept a marvelous supply of canned goods. These she ordered from S.S. Pierce & Company, a place down in Boston. She simply called them up and placed her order, and in another week or so the cans were delivered to her doorstep. Immediately Signe dated those cans. She had a walk-in cupboard built in the kitchen, with a wooden pullout step at the base of the wall. The cans dated, Signe pulled out that step and stood upon it to sweep the older cans to the front and place the new ones at the back. In these years since her death, this is what I have said of her: that she kept a marvelous supply of canned goods; that she never did find a suitor; and that she remains the bright pivot of my life.

It was Signe who raised me. At night, when she tucked me into bed in our house at 36 Highland Street, she would tell me the story of our family. They came over in the boat, she would say, with water for their blood. In my bedroom, a lightbulb with a circular shade made of birch bark hung from the ceiling. It turned slowly in the breeze and sent shards of dim light around the room. That refracted light made it seem as though Aunt Signe and I were together under the lake. On weekends we would walk there, to the lake, and from the pier Signe would point across to Bear Island. "Sophie, we two come from out there," she would say. "Your mother and father dropped beneath the ice and your grandmother turned wild on that wild island." It was a sad story, yet because I had no memory of anyone in it, the story was beautiful. It was the legend of my very own being, and it made me know that I belonged in this place.

I always believed that Signe, too, belonged in Kettleborough, though now I sometimes think she may have been better suited for city life. When I was a girl, she liked to take the train down to Boston. There we would go to the old Swedish church, where they still held an evening service in what Signe called the old language. And there was a man there. His name was Hjalmar, and his family had been close to Aunt Signe's father's family back in Sweden. They didn't say "Sweden," however; they referred to that place by sending an unspecific wave over their shoulder. The motion said that their country was not in fact a place, but something tucked away into time. In that gone-by time, Hjalmar had made a living as a tailor, yet here in America he was destitute. Signe would bring him bread wrapped in wax paper, and always a savory pie.

After church we three would walk together, and I vividly remember one of those walks. Night had fallen, and big, heavenly snowflakes fell down upon us. There must have been streetlamps, yet to me it seemed the snow itself illuminated the world. Hjalmar was a tall man, and he walked between us, his elbows hooked into ours. I felt wonderful with his arm in mine, protected and involved. When we passed a homeless man on the street, Hjalmar stopped and removed his wool coat. He gave it one firm shake. A wave passed slowly through the wool, and, once it was clean of snowflakes, Hjalmar draped that coat over the cold man.

"Hjalmar, your coat," my aunt said as we walked on.

"I can sew another," he said.

"You can't afford the wool for another," Signe said. It was a reprimand.

"That's right, too," Hjalmar said. His voice held no concern.

"Will you ask him to live with us?" I asked Signe that night, on the train ride home. She seemed astonished by my question. Yet if Hjalmar couldn't afford a coat, I didn't understand how he could afford to live at all.

"Don't you love him?" I asked. I must have said more. I knew that it was only when we traveled to see Hjalmar that Signe wore her pearl necklace and a bit of rouge on her cheeks. I must have made my meaning clear: Can't he be a husband to you?

"I cannot love Hjalmar as a woman loves a man," my aunt Signe said firmly. She kept her vision fixed on the dark night. I took her statement to mean that Hjalmar would not have her. And I understood to never suggest such a thing again.

My aunt was a teacher at the Kettleborough schoolhouse, and just across the street from that school, in the triangle made by the town's three roads intersecting, sat the Kettleborough Memorial Library. It was small. But it was also wonderful, made of brick, the south side a wall of buttresses and stained glass. Through that glass the sun shone in singular strands. The rest of the library was dark and musty, like an old stone castle, so those rays of colored light were striking. Signe, who loved nothing more than to stand in the sun with her eyes closed, used to enter the library, run her eyes over the small place, then walk with purpose to the book upon which the light directly fell. In this way she would decide what next to read.

"They never led to anything, those books," Signe said once, when I was grown. It wasn't until then that I understood that she had been on a search.

After school, Signe would cross the street to that library to visit the librarian. I didn't know the depth of their friendship, but it was clear to me that the librarian was my aunt's only friend in the area. It was a love of fashion that initially drew the two women together. Both were expert seamstresses, and their drooped necklines and high, fitted waistbands made them stand out in our small town. Though my aunt preferred muted tones, the librarian draped herself in vibrant colors, which certainly matched her personality. She was a joyful, unabashed woman whose husband stayed home to raise the children.

Not long after I asked Signe if she loved Hjalmar, the librarian gave my aunt a book. Signe came to my room with it in her hand. I was fourteen, and not a prude in matters of love. I don't know how Signe saw this, yet she was right; I had kissed and been groped by a few boys, and it was not something I felt any shame about. In fact, I enjoyed meeting boys in the dark of the boathouses that lined the lake. "This is my duty," Signe said, and sat at the edge of my bed. Nervousness had splotched her neck. After placing the book on my lap, she stood. Her straight back faced me. Her head was tilted slightly upward, so that her long rope of sandy hair reached her hips. Her hands, hanging awkwardly at her sides, continuously clenched and released. It wasn't the sort of motion my aunt typically made. She was a sure, firm woman.

"I know nothing of the subject," she finally said. "I have no experience with it." She kept pushing to make her meaning clear, though it certainly was to me. "None at all," she said. "But I do not wish such a fate upon you." When she left my room, Signe shut the door behind her. To shut a bedroom door was an action never taken in our small world.

When Signe was invited on her first date, I was there to witness it. It was at a town meeting. She had stood to make a plea: the school needed more money for books; all the copies of *Hamlet* were missing pages; the students couldn't be expected to learn in this way. When she took her seat again, Mr. John Perkins leaned over. "Dinner?" he whispered. In the summers, I was sent away to camp on the lake, and it wasn't until her old age that Signe admitted to me that in this time she had once attended a two-week charm school in Boston, and that twice she had gone on singles' cruises. It was the behavior she had learned during such events that I now witnessed—my strong aunt nodded her head downward, ever so slightly, and then held out her hand. We knew Mr. Perkins; people in our town knew one another. Yet her hand said she was pleased to make his acquaintance. "I'd be delighted," my aunt said. She mouthed the words, her lips full and her tongue soft upon her teeth. I was shocked.

They were to go to Pheasant View for dinner. It was on the outskirts of town, a place set high on the hill, with a stunning view of the lake. Signe prepared a fish pie for me, put it in the oven, and set the timer. She told me what time to put myself to bed. I did not have a bedtime, for I was a responsible teen who enjoyed living on the same schedule as my aunt. Also, she did not have to cook dinner for me; often I cooked for the two of us, and in fact we both knew that I had more of a talent for it than she did.

Hjalmar had given me a cookbook, the recipes written in both Swedish and English, and from it I loved to experiment. So I understood my aunt, on that night, to be intensely nervous. And I understood that it was not the date alone that she feared. In another year I would be off to college. My aunt, then, would be left alone. This date was a chance to find a companion. When she set out I lit a candle and said a small prayer. I wanted her to find a man to live with.

That night I stayed up late. I read poems aloud. I sat straight-backed in a chair, hands clasped together in my lap, and watched out the window for the two of them. It was fall and the maples were afire. In another thirty years or so, fall would become my hardest season, for in it my son would die when his car slipped on wet leaves, yet at that time it was my favorite. I believed, that night, that there was fate to the fact that Signe's very first date coincided with the change of seasons. I could not go to bed. I sat at the piano and played every hymn I knew, imagining, now and then, a life lived as a musician in the city. Finally, when my fingers could do no more, I went to the couch and fell asleep. Signe, when she came home in the early hours of morning, did not know I was there. The bathroom of that small house shared a wall with the living room, and in there I heard my aunt sobbing.

Virginity was something I had been taught that one loses, so it was over this loss that I felt my aunt must have been crying. And, in a way, I turned out to be right, for my aunt did sleep with that man. Yet it didn't happen in the way I imagined it. Before she died, when she had finally settled into her body and rid herself of shame, she admitted this to me. It had occurred in the car. She had kept her focus on the glimmering wing of a fly caught both in the vehicle and in a season that was past its own time. There had been no pleasure in his touch, yet she had pretended. "Oh," she had said. And, "I have never." She had been brave, to say that. And he had laughed.

On that night, I stayed on the couch until I was sure my aunt had fallen asleep. When I crept to my room, her own door was shut. Yet in the morning, Signe had decided to order a Monel metal sink. The Sears catalog was opened to the page; she was only waiting for me to wake and witness her extravagant purchase. She had a determined happiness about her.

"I will keep it shined at all times," she said. It came out like a wish.

Also on that morning, Signe did something else uncustomary for our routine life. It was Saturday, one of our two days together, and she left me alone.

All that day I walked idly from room to room. My aunt kept a collection of glass paperweights set deeply with various colors and designs, and I took them from the shelf one at a time and held them to the light in the window. It wasn't something I had ever done before. I wanted the color to spread across the room, yet nothing happened. The weights would not catch the sun, and I was left infinitely bored.

When Signe finally returned, she was in such a fit that her entrance startled me, and I dropped the weight that was in my hand upon the floor. It bounced, and though it did not split, when I picked it up I saw that a large chip was missing. In all my life, it was the only time I ever saw her furious. Yet when I began to apologize, I quickly saw that her anger had nothing to do with me. In her hands, Signe held a magazine, DISCARDED stamped in red across the cover. She threw it down upon the table, and I knew she had come from the library.

Banned, she told me of the magazine. It was one we had read together for years, which regularly featured stories and pictures from around the world, and this quarter it had arrived with the cover a picture of a woman nursing. Signe punched her hand upon it. The big, naked breast was the problem. "Hell!" she shouted. "Don't go telling me what I can read!"

The S.S. Pierce & Company catalog was in front of me, and while she circled the table in a storm, I began to look through it. From the drawer I took out a pad of paper and a pencil, and I began to make a list. Corn, tomatoes, green beans, peaches. It was the only thing I could think to do. "Wonderful," she said cruelly, when she saw my list. She took up the telephone and made her order. "Thank you, Mr. McCaffrey," she said, once she had finished reading. "Thank you for allowing me to order the food I want."

I don't know what Mr. McCaffrey said in response, but it must have been something remarkable, for suddenly an easy, pleasant-day sort of laugh burst forth from my aunt. "Thank you, Alexander," she said at the end of the call. A loud, long breath fell out of her and into the receiver. It was a breath of relief; her fit was over. "Yes," she said. "Good day, Alexander."

It was on the very next day that I pieced together why my aunt had been so furious: the Sunday paper arrived containing an open letter written by the librarian, and it revealed that Mr. Perkins, who only nights before had removed my own aunt's clothing, had been the one to insist that the naked breast was inappropriate.


Once in a while, Signe and I went a bit wild with our ordering. We bought all sorts of potted meats, and spices that seemed to us to be eccentric. Into our small house we brought pâté of pheasant, artichokes, English plum pudding, and peeled truffles. Now and again we supplied ourselves with expensive laundry soap or a collection of tapered candles. And sometimes, at the bottom of a list, in small, discreet letters, Signe would add one bottle of fine brandy.

*Grocery Department, Wine Department, Cigar Department, Per-*

*fumery Department,* the front of the catalog read. It was the last section that interested me the most. I could choose any scent— hibiscus, or perhaps bouquet Caroline—and match it with a product. There was bath oil, bath water, bath spray, even bar soap. When we made our list, I would always add one such choice to the bottom of the page. Yet never would my aunt order it, even though I had offered to pay with my own money, which I earned by doing a bit of garden work around the neighbor-hood. Signe was simply too modest to order such a personal, vain thing; in fact, when she got too old to bathe herself, and the task fell to me, she refused to remove her nightgown. Rather, she let it billow there in the tub. "Heaven forbid I should see you naked!" I would tell her each time. Without even the slightest hint of sarcasm, Signe would agree.

Yet one day my aunt, by mistake I am sure, ordered that last item on the list. It was a bottle of rose bath spray. By that time, we had ordered a great many things, and her friendship with Alex had gone on for nearly a year. I had noticed that before her calls, she would walk up and down the hallway two or three times, stopping at the mirror to adjust her bun or tighten her ponytail. Also by that time, the big cupboard had been built, and into this Signe would pull the telephone cord after her. "Why is it?" I asked her once. It was meant as a hint. I wanted to speak with her about love. "That when you call S.S. Pierce, you stretch that cord into the cupboard and shut the door after you?" Signe answered simply and quickly, saying she needed to see what we had and what we had room for. It was as though she had planned the response.

On the day that she mistakenly ordered the bath spray, Signe spoke with Alex for much longer than usual. I waited in the liv-ing room and now and again heard her laughter burst into the pages I was reading. After a considerable amount of time went by,

I rose and went to the kitchen for a glass of water, and it was then that I heard her say, rather loudly, just after "potted ham," that she would like one bottle of rose bath spray. Yet it was what she said next that shocked me more. "Yes," my aunt said. "I would be delighted if you would come visit me in Kettleborough."

On the weekend that he was to arrive, Signe prepared her specialty—meatballs, pickled and spiced beets, and even small cream-filled puff pastries. I had acquired a little makeup, and with hesitation Signe asked me in a quiet voice whether or not I could help her do herself up a bit. "Nothing that shows," she told me. I sat my aunt down on the edge of the bathtub and gently brushed powder across her cheeks and down the curve of her face to her neck. I gave one soft swipe across her forehead. I had her blink in order to line her lashes with a trace of mascara, and with my finger I rubbed a bit of deep pink paint against her lips. When I finished I backed up and looked upon her. My aunt had a long, regal face. From it she stared forward with such a strange mix of determination and gentle knowing that I was struck, and teared a little. I coughed to hide it. I don't think I had ever noticed it before, but my aunt was astonishingly beautiful.

Before setting out to the train station, she walked through the kitchen one last time with a towel in her hand. She rubbed one small spot off the sink. The entire place shone. I had told my aunt to go meet Alexander at the station on her own, but she refused, saying that it was important to the both of them that I come along. When we set out, arm in arm, I had the distinct feeling that our house would never be the same, which turned out to be true. He wasn't at the station. We waited for over an hour. We knew the train from Boston had already come and gone. We asked the ticket agent about a man who might have been looking for someone. When finally we walked home again, my aunt spoke plainly. Isn't the weather nice? she said. How I love the scent of freshly fallen leaves. At home, I removed the table setting we had put out for him, and put the blankets and pillow that we had set on the couch back into the hall closet. Call him, I suggested as I made my way back to the kitchen. Find out what has happened. Yet when I entered the kitchen I found my aunt silently pushing the dinner she had made into the trashcan. When she finished, she went to her room, lay down atop her quilt, and fell asleep in her pale yellow dress.

The next morning, Alexander called. He must have apologized. I do not know the explanation he gave my aunt for missing the train; I never asked. I was a devoted niece and did not want to bring up anything but happiness. Why she trusted him with her entire heart I did not know; in fact, at that time she, too, may not have known the reason for the connection they felt to each other in this big world. Yet she did trust him, and two more times my aunt and I walked together to the Kettleborough station on an early Friday evening to meet Alexander as he got off the train, and two more times Alexander did not appear.

"Wouldn't it be nice," my aunt told me around this time, "to go visit that church once again?" She meant the church in Boston, and I agreed. We put our dresses on, packed a thermos of coffee, a bag of crisp bread, and two apples, and boarded the train in Kettleborough. The ride was a quiet one. When we arrived, and Signe walked south rather than north, I asked her where it was that we were headed. She gave no reply, yet it wasn't long before I knew. S.S. Pierce & Company was set on a corner, in a building with a large clock tower and a Tudor pattern on the sides. That clock, when the building came into view, was just striking four in the afternoon. I do not think that Signe planned this journey; she was an honest woman, and I'm certain that she truly meant our trip to lead us to the church. Yet instead of going to the service, we walked back and forth outside of the building where Alexander would surely be.

When five o'clock struck, meaning that we had been pacing silently for an hour, I finally dared to ask my aunt if we shouldn't head over to the church. "You go if you like," she said. "I would rather like to return to Kettleborough." She was pale, her eyes set somehow more deeply into her face than usual. She looked terrified, and she carried a strong, pungent smell of sweat. I escorted her to the train station. Not long after we boarded, she fell asleep. It was the only time I had seen her act like that. I thought it pathetic, and I was filled with humiliation for her. That occurred in my last year of high school. The S.S. Pierce catalog was tucked into the back of the one messy drawer in the house, the place where we kept all the odds and ends that never seemed to have a logical place. I took to buying our groceries at the store. Though our meals were not as elaborate as they had once been, we were certainly nourished.

After that last year of high school, I left for the summer to head north, to the mountains, where I had a job working at a grand hotel. It wasn't a difficult decision to make; both Signe and I knew this. I had recently been accepted to a college in Boston and would leave in the fall. Though this summer job sped up my departure by three months, it also provided me with enough spending money to last through my entire first year of college. And it would give me—though I wouldn't know it for a few years to come—the opportunity to meet the man who would become my husband. So this time, when Signe and I went to the train station, I boarded alone, and she returned to an empty, shining house.

I was in the hotel kitchen when I received a call from the Kettleborough librarian. I was with the man I would one day marry—Otto was his name—and we were folding cloth napkins into bird-like shapes that would stand on their own in the center of the plates. There were large windows in the kitchen, and directly outside stood Mount Washington, bald and peaked with snow. I was used to the big lake, which allowed me to look out across the world and receive some feeling of expanse. Yet this mountain, which was the biggest, roughest I had ever seen, stood there in my line of vision like a great wall and left me feeling as if the only path for us to pursue was upward. It was a kind of religious feeling, though I didn't understand what that amounted to. Otto was a silly man, and he had tucked his hands into two white napkins to make a sort of puppet out of them, and with a surprising talent for ventriloquism he was making these napkins speak. When a voice from the intercom interrupted us, I thought we had been caught in our fooling while on the clock. I was called to the office. Otto walked with me, a gentleman ready to take the blame. Yet in the office I was given a number and told simply to phone the Kettleborough library. As I dialed, I looked out upon that big mountain and prayed for it to keep my aunt unharmed.

"How long," the librarian wanted to know, "will it take you to get yourself home?"

Since guests usually asked such questions, the hotel kept the train schedule taped next to every phone. In less than three hours I could be in Kettleborough.

"Come quickly," the librarian said. "Meet me at the pier."

I remember that after I hung up the telephone, I asked that mountain directly, aloud, to please let Signe be safe. Later, Otto would tell me that it was at that strange moment, when he was a witness to my unexplainable faith, that he decided to marry me. He carried my bag to the train station and placed a small kiss upon my hand. That ride could have been days and it could have been minutes; I only stared forward.

The Kettleborough train stops right at the pier, and before I even set foot outside, I could tell that there was some commotion in the water. Perhaps a mile from shore there was a cluster of rowboats, and on the pier a group of perhaps ten or fifteen people stood, the librarian one of them. From the train I ran to her. She promptly shuffled me into a small motorboat, and together we made our way across the water.

It was Signe who was out there. Our lake sits in the vast valley made by that northern range of mountains, so all those miles away, the big mountain I had prayed to was still in view. Behind it the sun had just dropped. Darkness would come soon. Signe was on her back, in all her clothing. Her skirt billowed and the white fabric of her shirt exposed her undergarments. Her hair was beautifully fanned about her head. The lake was not calm; in fact, it was filled with whitecaps. Her eyes were opened but they might as well have been closed, for there was no expression upon her face. Her arms were spread outward. The men in the rowboats were calling her name. They had tried to jump in and retrieve her, but each time, my aunt put up a solid, silent fight. Already she had broken the nose of one man. "You'll drown her," the librarian had finally said. "Or you'll make her drown herself." It was the librarian who had insisted they call me and wait.

"Signe," I called from the boat. She didn't move. "Signe," I kept saying. Finally I had the sense to tell all those others to leave, and I dove into the water. I swam to her, and just then the sun suddenly and impossibly peaked above that high mountain in one quick burst. My aunt, in that second, shone as if she alone provided the light of the world.

"Oh, Sophie," she said simply, once the sun had returned to its normal state. "It's you." She flipped onto her stomach and swam the sidestroke to shore. Dripping wet, she walked out of the water, up the pier steps, across town, and to our house. She held her head high.

.  .  .

In anticipation of my absence and her solitude, she had, by that time, separated the Highland house into two apartments. It was a rather simple construction. The upstairs she now rented out to a young couple who had just come to the area, and the downstairs she reserved for herself. Signe went in, and I followed. There was a path of water from the doorstep across to the kitchen sink and then into the bathroom. Yet more shocking than that carelessness was the clothing—every last garment that Signe owned had been scattered about the apartment. All of it, the couch and chairs and dining room table, was covered in her slim dresses, her long, pleated skirts, and her organdy blouses. Even her evening gown, a stunning dress of chiffon that she had sewn but never worn, was thrown on the table. Her bed was also covered, and upon it my soaking aunt lay. Her mouth hung open. She had already fallen asleep. Gently I removed her wet clothes and covered her with a blanket from the closet. She didn't rise for another three days. In this time I stayed with her, slept next to her on the bed, fed her. And, once, when I went out to set the trash on the curb, rather than going back into her house I climbed up the wooden stairs they had built as an entrance to the upstairs apartment and knocked on the door. A young woman answered; she must have been a year or two older than I. Her hair was dyed a bright blond, and she held a baby in her arms. She had a wonderfully unsure smile, as if she thought she ought to be happy, but wasn't quite positive about why. I told her that I just wanted to introduce myself, that I had lived in that house all my life, that I was grateful to meet her. She must have taken me for Signe's daughter, for she said, "I have met Alexander this past weekend. Is he your father?"

When Signe finally woke and sat up, I mustered the courage to ask her if Alex had indeed come to see her.

"Oh, yes," she said. She said it as though it was the plainest occurrence in the world.

My aunt could have died out there in the lake; I felt I had no choice but to be blunt. "Signe," I asked, "did he break your heart?"

To my question she laughed a long, uncontrollable laugh. For a moment I felt she was mocking me, yet her laughter was much too true for that. "Oh," she finally said. "It was the brandy that has done it." After that she simply stood up, crossed the room, and went to the bathroom. There she drew herself a bath. When that was finished, she began to sing a loud Swedish country song, and she put a blue, flowing, water-like dress on. She walked about the house as though it was Sunday and she had not a care in the world. Never again did she mention that weekend.

Yet she did take to saying, now and then, "It was the brandy that has done it." She said this at odd, exhausted, happy times, and in my small understanding of her, I believed she had gone a bit crazy. For she had changed. Become, in a sense, freer, looser, her motions now sweeping and her laughter unkempt. I believed it was my aunt's only way of coping. I knew her rules. Signe took only one swig of brandy at a time, either to calm her nerves or to put herself to sleep. She was not a woman to alter her own rules. That man had forced her, I decided. Alexander McCaffrey had forced my dear aunt.


That year, on a Friday afternoon after my courses in Boston, I boarded a trolley and rode over to the Pierce building. Just as Signe had walked up and down that street, I now paced there like an obsessed woman. When the bell struck to mark an hour's time passing, I entered the building. I had practiced what I would say. I told the woman working the front desk that I would like to speak with Alexander McCaffrey. As she flipped through a circular address reel, I became sure that she would say no man of such a name worked there. Yet she gave me directions to his cubby. It wasn't but two doors down the hallway. He would be in the fifth desk on the right. "It's the man who takes the orders from Kettleborough, New Hampshire?" I asked. She assured me that it was.

In that hallway I lost what I would say, and I went back out again for fresh air. In winter, in our part of the country, a gray darkness settles early upon us. In that darkness, with the voices of the people passing before me somehow distant, I suddenly thought of Hjalmar. To die alone in this cold place, I thought. As it turned out, Hjalmar had died of cold, as Signe had worried he would. I learned this when, as Signe had said, I was old enough to not frighten myself with it. I also learned that when he had lost his apartment she had in fact asked him to live with us, and she had also given him a fair amount of money, both of which he had refused. That coat, I recalled when Signe told me the story, could have saved his life. Yet to regret giving it was something I was sure Hjalmar never did.

I walked back into that building. I tapped the man's shoulder, and asked him if he truly was Alexander McCaffrey. He had a head of soft, neatly brushed hair, and his fingers were long. The nails, I noticed, were clean and well cut. His top lip, which I imagined would be nothing more than a cliff that dropped sharply into his mouth, was round and full and deeply cleft. That face: he could have been a boy. He stared up at me as if he had been caught. How I must have scared that poor man. His secret was revealed, he must have thought with a terror. For the truth, I would learn, was simple: Alexander McCaffrey was a gay man, and only my aunt Signe knew.

"I know what you have done to my poor aunt," I said with conviction. And Alex, of course he lied.

"Signe?" he said. "I do not know a Signe. Kettleborough? No, I've never been there."

His bottom lip slipped into his mouth and he sucked on it the way a baby might. Any passerby would have known he was lying. Yet I could say nothing in reply.


In her last years, we packed Signe's things and moved her into my family's house on the hill. On good days she turned opera on in the kitchen and walked from room to room with her arms waving, as though from her own limbs the sounds came forth. On neutral days she read, and there were not many bad days, even at the very end. Into our house, along with her bags, I had also carried the bravery to bare all I could to Signe before she died, and to ask for all I wanted. What happened? I asked her one day, as she sat in her living room chair, her eyes open wide to the sunlight that poured in upon her. What I meant to ask was what had happened on that day that she had drifted so far out in the lake. What happened with Alexander to cause her to do that, I wanted to know.

"My heavenly days," she said. The words rolled fully from her lips. She clapped her hands together and I knew that in her mind she was drifting far away. "Go to the drawer," she said after some time. I knew which drawer she meant; it was in one of the only pieces of furniture she had brought in the move, and it was where the catalog had been kept. "An envelope," she said. "March fourteen I believe it says." That date was my aunt's birthday. It took me a while to find the envelope. I had to pull the drawer out from the table and empty its contents one at a time. There were shoelaces and pens, old photographs, a protractor. Tucked into the first page of the S.S. Pierce & Company catalog is where I found the envelope. It didn't say March 14. Rather, Signe had written in careful handwriting, *On my 60th birthday.* I brought it to her. She was in her mid-eighties now, her hands shaky and her dark veins showing through her thin, aged skin. I had to help her open the envelope. A newspaper article was tucked inside. The ink smudged on her fingers and when she wiped at her hair she left a black streak on her forehead. The article was about Alexander. On her sixtieth birthday Signe had gone, she told me, down to Boston to see her friend. She had imagined it as a surprise gift, for after he told her his secret, they had made a pact to not speak again. It wasn't shame, she said, but some sort of horror. Some acceptance of the long, lonely life to come. "We had simply understood," she said. "It seemed the way it had to be." Yet after nearly twenty years of honoring that pact, on that birthday Signe gathered her courage. As she walked toward S.S. Pierce she imagined the way they would talk. How they would laugh, eat a long, slow dinner. They would look back upon their lives, the way they had turned out, not so bad at all. It wasn't until she made her way over to the Pierce building that she looked at the newspaper. Alexander McCaffrey had fallen into the Boston channel, and after a week his body had been found and identified. "He fell," the witness had insisted. "Sure as day that man fell."

"With that secret," my aunt said now, "you do not fall into the channel."

It took me some time to understand what she was telling me. When I finally grasped it I went on. I said, "Can you imagine? Can you imagine knowing, your entire life, that you would fit nowhere? That you had no one to tell your secret to?" For though by this time the troubles of my life had seemed insurmountable, hearing Alex's story somehow pulled me out. I had given and received love, after all.

"Why yes," my aunt said. She sounded both forceful and

astonished. "Yes," she said, "I can understand perfectly well what Alexander McCaffrey went through." She held out her hand for me to return the newspaper clipping. She was angry. Which, for my dim-wittedness, she had every right to be. She must have thought that I knew—always had known—and respected her own secret. She must have felt as I did—that we two knew each other as well as any two people could. But all those years, I had failed to understand that she herself was a gay woman. "I can understand every last bit of it," she said sharply.

I never did find out what exactly my aunt meant to do on that day in the lake. For years I supposed that after her time with Alexander she had simply stood on the pier and allowed her mind to go blank, and that in that state she had been called back to that island she had come from. Though I have never acted upon it, that is what I have felt many times as I look out toward Bear Island, that wild and solitary place.

For her death, I dressed Signe in an ivory-colored organza gown with sleeves that would flutter. I pinned flowers at her waist. For a ball, tea, maybe a wedding, Signe had said when she sewed that dress. She never completed it; I found it at the back of her closet, and it was I who made the final stitches.

"She lived a long life," the librarian said as we stood together outside the small church after Signe's funeral. She wrapped her arms tightly around me. "Thank God for that," she said. "Thank God she never did go through with it."

Then she told me that Alexander and Signe had eaten a wonderful dinner together when he finally did visit, and together they shared a bottle of brandy. For two nights they slept beside each other on Signe's bed. In a way it was the brandy that had done it, for it allowed them to expose themselves. When Alexander boarded the train, it was down that long track that my aunt looked, and what she saw was the endless stretch of her lonely life. She hadn't been called to the island. Instead, she had been called to the shore, down by the town docks, where old rope and rocks were piled. My aunt wrapped the rocks with that old rope. Next she tied the rope around her ankles. I don't know how far she made it out into the water in this way. I don't know if the knots were poorly tied or the rope too loose, or if a sweep of something greater than herself came across her mind to make her reach under and untie those rocks. But she did, and once they dropped to the floor of our lake my aunt rose, gasping, and it was her rising that the librarian witnessed. She tried to call Signe in but she would not come. Did my aunt mean to continue with her plan, to drift out and die simply in the middle of the lake? I wonder that sometimes, but I suppose it doesn't matter. What matters is that the sun suddenly, impossibly, burst forth above that big mountain far away, that it and the lake embraced my aunt, and that my aunt swam home.

# Hush

## 1958

OH GLORY BE, Sophie thought on September 16, 1958, when her son brought the infant home. This small being, the world is good. She held the baby to her chest and ran a soft finger down the stretch of her forehead, along the ridge of her nose, and then, knowing it would comfort her son, she handed that gleaming new body back to him. Without the baby in her arms Sophie's hands gripped the porcelain sink once more. Behind her, her husband sat slumped at the kitchen table, his cheek right there against the maple, not even his arms to shield himself.

"My heavenly days," she said softly, her vision cast out the window. There were turkeys out there, one mother with eight little ones in tow. When the mother perched on the stone wall, one by one the others did the same, and when Malcolm looked out the window he saw all the turkeys sitting at ease, sunning themselves on the Wickholm land. It wasn't until a car crested the driveway and the turkeys skittered away that Sophie turned to her thirteen-year-old son and asked, "Malcolm, whose baby have you got?"

She might have been asking him what picture show he'd seen that week, for her words came out that unremarkably. As did this: "Malcolm, your brother is dead."

Once she'd said it, Sophie sat down, took one long, deep breath, straightened her back, and clasped her hands together in her lap. Her Karl. He had worked for two years to save for that Ford that he had bought himself, and then he had driven the Ford for one year, and then he had rounded a corner too fast on wet leaves and hit a tree and died. Malcolm said nothing. He simply lifted the infant higher on his shoulder, patted her back, and carried her up the stairs. In his bedroom he made a bed of blankets on the hardwood floor. He laid her down and began to sing, "Row, row, row your boat." His voice cracked and teetered. The baby was sleeping, had been since the moment he found her, perhaps one hour ago. With nothing left to do for her, Malcolm walked down the stairs, but seeing neighbors with casseroles, he walked back up, and seeing the baby still sleeping, he walked back down, and in this manner he passed the rest of the day, and most of the next.

It would be another few years before Aunt Signe sold her own home and moved in with her niece, but in the days after Karl's death she came each day to see that life in the Wickholm house continued to move forward. Despite the fact that she was so old that her back hunched when she walked and her arms shook when she lifted anything, it was Aunt Signe who went to the store for formula and bottles, and she who went to the attic to find the cloth diapers that Sophie's own children had worn. It was also Aunt Signe who said to Sophie's husband, "Otto, you know where that baby came from."

The boathouse, that was the answer Malcolm had given. Originally it had just been a shed built over the water, a place for Otto to store his motorboat and, eventually, Malcolm's canoe. But a few years back Otto had followed the pattern of so many others in town and had a second level built above the first, which he rented out as an apartment. The baby, Malcolm said, had been in the lower level, in the floating canoe. He said it was a miracle clear as day that she hadn't been tossed into the whitecapped water. When he said this Sophie went to him, patted his hair, and told him she agreed.

Otto didn't say a word, not to Signe and not to anyone else. Instead, in his own way, he went a little mad. In response to Signe's statement he walked out of the house and down to his shop in town, where he made and sold ice cream, as his father and grandfather had. He spent the night there, and many more after that. On the first night he made more ice cream than he had ever made before—one hundred gallons; he simply started with it and could not stop. After that he took a rest on the cement floor and then he began again, making and freezing ice cream and making and freezing more. He would never be able to sell it all, and he was already running out of room to store it. Still he kept on, and on the rare occasions that he did return home, he kept his eyes averted from the baby. It wasn't difficult to do, because each time he entered the house Sophie or Malcolm would scoot that baby right up the stairs, out of sight.

. . .

Aunt Signe washed and pressed the laundry, cleaned the house, cooked the food, and tended to the bills. And, more than once, she said to her niece, "I should expect you intend to claim that child."

At first, Sophie, like her husband, gave no response. One time she said yes. The final time, though, she kept her eyes fixed out the window, on those turkeys in the yard, as she said to her aunt that they both knew the sort of husband Sophie had chosen. "But Otto is a good man," she said lightly.

And Otto was good, or at least he firmly meant to be. But he had been raised in a certain way; his mind had formed in a certain way. Things were right or things were wrong and if he could not decide which it was, he figured he'd best do away with it. In town he kept watch in the papers and listened on the streets and in the post office, trying to see if anyone knew about the baby. He heard nothing, and at times he wondered if perhaps it could just continue in this secret way. So he would let his wife have what she wanted. He could just stay away. Because to speak up— no, look at the life he had built, the values he stood for. But to take the baby from her, surely that would break his dear Sophie in half.

The Wickholms' house sat on the top of the hill, higher than any other in Kettleborough, with a grand view of the lake below. The only thing that obstructed the view was the Randolph house and the clump of pines on the Randolph land. Otto had wanted those trees cut down. He had even offered to pay for the job to be done, but Mrs. Randolph had sent her oldest son up to their house to tell them no. "They're Mother's favorites," the boy had stood on the porch repeating as though it were the only sentence he knew. Now Otto walked past those trees, past that house with its paint peeling and its lawn overgrown and its yard so overrun with junk that it could be taken for the dump itself, past Mrs. Randolph, who sat glued, as always, to her rocking chair on the porch. He kept his shoulders high, his eyes pointed toward his own tall white home, just ten or so yards above.

"Evening, Otto!" Mrs. Randolph hollered, as she always did.

Otto tipped his head in her direction. Typically that marked the end of the interchange. But now she whistled to him and called out, "Not so fast." As usual, she had that telephone in her lap, that long, curly cord stretched out from her kitchen. That Mrs. Randolph passed the day away by listening in on neighbors' phone calls was no secret.

Otto wouldn't stop for her. Instead he gave a firm salute and continued walking up the hill. He was still within earshot when he heard her say, "I knows about that child. Don't go thinking I don't."


"One more day," Sophie pleaded when her husband marched into the house, told her that the baby had to go and there would be no discussion about it, and then marched right back out. The door had already closed after him by the time her words came out.

"You know how to be the person I raised," Signe said.

"Jennifer," Sophie said in response. "Someone has to call Jennifer."

With his father out of the house, Malcolm knew he had to do it. He went to his father's office and took up a pen and wrote Jennifer's name in that big, bubbly script she had used. He wrote the number, too—he knew it by heart. Everyone in the family did. For though Jennifer was a Hill—which even Malcolm understood to mean that she was of the poorest class of people in Kettleborough—she had become a part of the Wickholm family. Karl had met her out at summer camp two years ago and the two had been in love ever since. "That girl is smart," Otto had liked to say, "but not from a good family." "That's a hard worker, but not from a good family." She had been one of the girls who went to summer camp for free, which Malcolm knew because his father had told him as if in answer to his question, which had simply been, "Why is she allowed to sleep at our house?"

But then not four months ago Jennifer had stopped coming over.

Malcolm dialed. Jennifer's mother answered.

"Karl has died," Malcolm said quickly. It was that word, *died*. It had been two weeks. That word was too soon. "My brother," he went on. "This is Karl Wickholm. Malcolm Wickholm I mean. My brother. Jennifer's boyfriend." He stopped and took a deep breath, wiped his arm across his sweating brow. "My mother asked me to call," he finally admitted.

"I'll be," the woman said.

What kind of mother would this woman be, to keep a home that wasn't good? Malcolm had never thought to ask.

"What is your name?" he said now. It felt adult, that question.

"Valerie. Val, people call me."

"Do you have a husband?"

"Are you interested?" The woman laughed. Her voice was husky. Malcolm imagined an angular glass of whiskey and ice in her hand. "I'm sorry, honey," she said after a moment. "A joke. My Jennifer's gone missing, you know that? I was hoping she was over there in your house, but she's not. I know your Karl's dead. Mrs. Randolph called us up."


Malcolm found his mother in his own bedroom. She was sitting on the floor, the baby between her outstretched legs. In her hands danced ribbons of red and pink, which she'd curled with the edge of scissors. The baby squirmed toward the ribbon and made her wonderful infant noises.

"Jennifer has gone missing. Did you know? Her mother knows Karl is gone. Mrs. Randolph called her up. They're friends, did you know? She was listening in, Mrs. Randolph, I heard the click of the phone."

Sophie clapped her hands and gave the baby a wink to tell her it would be all right, which of course it would not. Jennifer gone missing, there was the proof. What lengths would Otto go to, if she ignored his orders and allowed this to go on? She clapped once more and looked about the room. She had always meant to put new wallpaper up in here. Would Karl remember what his room had looked like? No, that is not what she meant. What does a dead person remember. I remember roller-skating on the marvelous cement sidewalk, Sophie thought. There now. If her Karl had lived, that is what she meant. If he had lived would it have been the cold jumps into the lake on the first day of summer? The cookies warm from the oven, his first love?

"We've got to do something about this baby," Sophie scolded her son. "Call Joseph at the fire station. Find out what happens to a baby without a home. Get the Polaroid. Call Joseph and get the Polaroid."

Malcolm did as he was told. With the camera in his hand he had to wait some time on the line while the men at the fire station bickered. Mrs. Randolph was listening in and it must have been excruciating for her to keep silent, for certainly she knew the answer to the question. Clara and Paul Thorton is what Joseph came back to say. They were the foster parents for Kettleborough.

"Can't we . . . ," Malcolm said hopelessly to his mother. He had not begun to piece things together. He simply loved the baby.

"Hush," she said. She held the baby in her arms and had Malcolm snap a picture. Then she took one with her son holding the child. Finally she took a picture in which Malcolm held the baby forward, so that only her own little body dangled there in the frame.

"Hide these upstairs," she said. Again he agreed, because he had not seen his mother behave in such a rushed manner before. When he came back she instructed him to put his father's large coat on and drape the edge of it over the child. "Don't need Mrs. Randolph seeing us, now do we?" she said.

They walked down the hill and into town. Malcolm kept his nose pressed against the fuzzy head of the child. That smell, he could inhale it for a lifetime. The Thortons lived just across the street from the library, in a little red carriage house with a stone wall to line the front. Sophie and Malcolm took their time walking up the drive. They stood on the granite step and breathed that wood smoke and fallen leaf smell and it was Malcolm who finally raised his arm and knocked.

"We have found a baby," he said.

Clara said she couldn't just take a baby like this. "There will have to be an investigation," she said.

Sophie shuddered then. A small, faint shudder that Malcolm imagined was just the noise of a wild animal, like a bear or a deer, when it has a few breaths to go but knows that after that its lifetime of breath will be used up.

Malcolm straightened his back and handed the baby Clara's way, then ironed his coat with his hands. "The police have very recently delivered heartbreaking news to our home," he said in a steady voice. "My mother does not wish to deal with the police. You will understand."

"Yes," is all Clara said. Her husband came to the door and Malcolm shook his hand.

"We can't just take a baby like this," Paul said to Malcolm.

But they took her anyway. Alice, she would soon be called, and in another couple of weeks news would come that the Thortons had decided to adopt her as their own. Now, on the way up the hill, Malcolm assured his mother that they were good, quiet people and that they would care well for that baby.

Some days Sophie played slow piano songs that contained a glimmer not of hope or of happiness but of something akin to both. These chords rose out of a place like old age, wherein the player could see or smell the tip of a memory, but she could not grasp on to the image enough to say what it was she remembered and anyway if it belonged to her. These songs were Malcolm's favorites.

Other days Sophie played the songs from just after the war ended. Back then she dressed in shorter skirts than she had ever worn before, and how she danced, and the parties! For an entire summer they would be booked up one Saturday after another. "Bring someone home with you for dinner," she would tell her husband. Now there was no one, not even Signe, for the two of them had had their first fight. It was over a deed to a small plot of land and a run-down cabin out on the island they had both come from—Signe believed that in the least, the girl ought to have that one day. Sophie didn't disagree, not entirely, but to Signe she had heard herself say, "We best make a clean break of it." It was an awful, shameful thing to say, and now she felt sure that it wasn't what had been in her heart. But Signe had left straightaway, and when she called later that day it was only to say that she had given the deed and all the necessary paperwork to Clara Thorton, who had been instructed to see that it was passed on to the girl when she came of age. Now nearly a week had passed and Signe had not reappeared.

But the hymns, these would keep Sophie going. She thought she knew at least two hundred of them. Hear a song one time, and she could play it straight through. It was a gift and in the days after the baby Sophie sat at her piano and wondered what it might mean to leave this life for another. A musician in the city, a real, independent woman—she could become that; she believed she could. But instead she stayed at home and felt like the most horrible mother ever to be put upon this earth and she kept her suffering to herself, for that is the way it was done. Each time the mailman came to the front step and dropped a letter addressed to Malcolm from Jennifer in Oregon through the slot, Sophie would watch it as though it could at any moment move of its own volition. She would watch the dust in the air gleam in the sunlight and she would lift one of her aunt Signe's glass paperweights from the mantel and hold it to the sun, trying, with no success, to make the beams of light refract, and she would know that her son was down the hill visiting the baby at Clara and Paul's, and she would finally, when the letter did not move, stand up and say, "Make something of this blessed life," and she would take that letter and hide it in the pile at the back of her top dresser drawer, where those pictures were, too, and she would return to the piano.

Because what was her son to do with the words from Jennifer? What weight might those words pass on to him? There were two letters now and Sophie had not opened either of them, but she had held them to the light in the window, to no avail.

But thank goodness for the turkeys. First that small family and now they had joined forces. Seven adults and twenty-three children, thirty turkeys in all! Daily they came into the field to sun themselves. "I could not go to the store," Sophie had heard herself tell Otto one day. It was the first sentence she had spoken to him since they had handed the baby over. "I could not go out, it would disturb the turkeys." The moment she said it she wished she had kept it to herself. Not to punish Otto; Sophie wasn't the sort for that. This silence she now existed in had just washed over her. Maybe, she thought now, it was to punish herself. She had done wrong and so she would be silent. She would just go along, care for the turkeys. Do turkeys eat apples? There were four apple trees out there in the field and each year since her marriage Sophie had made enough applesauce to last through winter, but this year look at all those fallen apples. They were rotting out there among the leaves, which Malcolm had not raked because he had decided that he liked the look of it as it was, and Sophie had known just what he meant.

Stand up. Do something with yourself. Sophie went out and placed apple after fallen apple into the wheelbarrow. She dumped them all near the stone wall, at the edge of the trees, an offering for the turkeys. When that was done morning had passed, and she reached up to pick her first apple. She bit in and that was joy, simple and quick. Sophie picked all the apples off the trees that day, and when she brought them inside she smothered the couch with them. Now she would make her applesauce; she would fill the house with that smell that told her sons that this was a place to come in and sit down and be home. Her son, she meant. Just the one.

By the time Sophie had boiled down a batch of apples and cranked it through the food mill, there were footsteps outside and then the clank of the mail slot. Oh heavens, not another. Sophie lifted the pot and walked from the stove to the living room and saw that letter gleaming there on the floor. She released her grip and the pot clanged against the wooden floor and the sauce pooled at her feet. She walked upstairs without picking up the letter, and when Malcolm came home he found a trail of pink, and in that trail a letter from sweet Jennifer.

．　　．　　．

Malcolm stood in his driveway, watching the lake and dreaming of a life lived out on that wild island. He had never been there. But he could go! He could pack his things and steal that beautiful baby and he could paddle the three miles out to Bear Island and live there, as his ancestors had done. Hunt deer and build a house and use cattails to keep his fishing holes open through winter.

"Malcolm!" he heard. "Malcolm!" It was Mrs. Randolph. She wanted him to come to her porch. He had never been invited there before and though it was not something his father would have allowed, Malcolm marched her way.

"Sit," Mrs. Randolph ordered.

Oh, it did smell wonderful out here. That cold air and that wood smoke, those gone-by leaves. He could see why she would spend all her time outside. And maybe he could stay with her. For just last week when Malcolm had entered his own home he had heard his mother say to Aunt Signe that when Malcolm was out of the house her Karl was every bit as present as living Malcolm was. So he would stay away. That was a small thing that hurt terribly but still a small thing he could give his mother.

Malcolm kept his hands in his pockets and looked on at Mrs. Randolph, rocking in her chair. She wasn't old, not from up close. No older than his own mother. She wore jeans and a man's flannel shirt, a man's pair of slippers. Her hair was parted bluntly down the middle and her skin was dark and rough. Malcolm sat below her, on the peeling steps, and she said nothing and he said nothing for a long while. Then the floorboards creaked from inside the house, and the screen door slowly opened. It was her youngest son, who held the door open with his foot while he reached to hand a mug of coffee to his mother.

"And I didn't even ask!" she hollered to him. It wasn't but another moment before the floorboards creaked once more and her son reappeared. This time he handed a cup of coffee down to Malcolm, and then disappeared inside.

"I had a brother died, too," Mrs. Randolph said as Malcolm took his first sip. His tongue burned and heat spread throughout his chest. He had never had coffee like this before, thick and silty.

"Jesse Hill," she continued. "Did you know I'm a Hill by birth? Must be some Hills in your class. Nathan? Tammy? Jesse died out in the lake. It ain't easy all I'm saying."

"No," Malcolm said.

"So there it is. Now we knows something about each other." A cough came out of her from the depths and sent her body into three solid convulsions.

Malcolm said, when she was finished, "Yes."

"So what you going to do about Karl's child?"

"Sorry?"

"You heard me."

Malcolm reached to place the half-finished mug of coffee on the edge of the porch but missed. It dropped to the ground and spilled. He picked it up but misplaced it again, and it fell once more.

"Leave it," Mrs. Randolph finally said.

He did, and down the hill toward the lake he ran.


*Dear Malcolm,*

*In school they teach you to say Or-e-gone, but out here I learned fast they say Or-e-gen. How are things at home? Do you know how long this country stretches flat? One day you will take a train across and you will see what I mean. I am in the mountains now. I have taken a job on a farm and I have my own apartment. It's really a*

*room and a loft to sleep in, attached to the landladies' house. They're*
*lovers. My place has a small table and two wicker-backed chairs*
*and a woodstove and a stove to cook on. The whole place is old and*
*wooden. It reminds me of your home and your mother. How is your*
*mother?*

*We take care of goats here. Usually they have their babies in the*
*spring but this year the ladies say something is off, and everything is*
*late. They say they cannot understand it. Anyway, when a mother*
*is ready to have her baby we have to lock her up in her own pen so*
*that the other goats don't get a chance to hog all her food. The baby*
*goats are so wonderful, Malcolm. I hold my finger out and they*
*grab right on and suck. Their little mouths and their little legs make*
*me feel so happy. We have to take them from their mothers. Did you*
*know that's how it works? It's so that we can steal the mother's milk*
*and drink it ourselves and sell it. The first goat I had to steal was*
*Buttercup, and I cried when I did it. She's the runt of a litter. I want*
*to take her up to my apartment and raise her myself.*

*The landladies had me for goat stew last night. I did not want*
*to eat it. My legs shook under the table. In the night I woke up*
*screaming, sure that a large windowpane was breaking upon my*
*head. I will not eat goat again.*

*Do you remember how I used to go to church with you? Will you*
*please speak to me about religion? I don't know how to say anything*
*about your brother. I loved him, too, and I hope your family is okay.*

*Love, Jennifer*

"Well, isn't that something." It was the sort of thing his father
would say. Malcolm tapped the letter against his thigh and then
moved to place it in his breast pocket, only to realize that he did
not have such a pocket. "Well," he said again. The telephone
rang and he knew his mother would not answer it because daily

she moved further and further from this world that Malcolm occupied.

It was his father on the line, wanting Malcolm to prepare a Thanksgiving dinner. Of course there would be no one to invite, not so close to the holiday. No one but Aunt Signe, whom Malcolm really ought to call for help, but did not, for he had been taught to not be a burden.


*Dear Malcolm,*

*The windows of the place where I live look out to a big meadow. That's what they call it out here, they call a field a meadow. When I first came here the meadow was covered in yellow. Buttercups, those were the flowers. You know them. We have them in Kettleborough, too. When I saw the meadow like that, all yellow, my first thought was that a painter had swept his paintbrush across it. This morning when I woke up I looked out the window to see that it had all gone purple. Like the painter came in the night to repaint the meadow. I asked the landladies about the flowers, but now I can't remember their name. They say that this year, like everything else, the flowers are so late, but that before the snow falls the meadow will be repainted blue.*

*It is a high elevation here. The weather is not like other places. The apricot tree outside my window bloomed in pink blossoms that fell down like rain when the wind blew, but now the blossoms are coated with ice. Buttercup, the goat I told you about, would not take to the bottle. Now I have vowed to never drink goat milk. Had we not been so selfish with her mother's milk, Buttercup would have survived. Last night it froze, and Buttercup's life ended.*

*If you can, please tell your mother I love her.*

*Love, Jennifer*

*Malcolm,*

*There are dogs here that are big and fluffy. They are not allowed inside the house. Instead their job is to sleep all day and then circle the property at night to guard the livestock. They bark through the whole night, but it does not bother me. Do you know how it is to sleep close to our lake, and listen to the waves against the shore? It feels like that. But last night I woke up to the most terrible sounds. At first I thought it was my own screaming. But when I sat up I knew that the sounds were of something dying. And then I fell right back to sleep. Isn't that strange? I keep thinking of it. I sat up, I knew that something was dying, and I lay back down. It's cold here at night, and I keep a fire in the woodstove. All the heat drifts to the loft, and I get so hot.*

*When I woke up I remembered what I had heard and I looked out the window. In the meadow there was one of the dogs. She stayed there all day. Sleeping by her kill, the landladies told me. A deer had crossed into the meadow and headed for the barn, and that dog had killed her.*

*I think of death a lot here. In the barn I have to open the hatch on the second floor to throw hay down to the goats, and I always imagine myself falling through the hatch and breaking my neck. There are two sows here that are huge and pregnant, and when I climb into their pen with the pitchfork to muck it out, I see myself tackled and eaten. It could happen easily enough.*

*The truth is that I keep hoping for a letter from you. You can give my address to your mother if you want. You can show her the letters if you want. Forgive me for my mistakes.*

*Love, Jennifer*

The first freeze of the year had come a few weeks ago, and now, in the evening sunlight, the moss on the rocks sparkled with a wet cold. Malcolm walked slowly through the cemetery before heading to the grocery store. Karl's ashes, Malcolm knew, were still in a box in his mother's bedroom. The name was typed and pasted to the top of the box: KARL OTTO WICKHOLM. Upon this box Sophie kept a pile of fresh laundry, a way to spare her husband. Malcolm hadn't said anything, but he wanted a stone put here, in the Kettleborough graveyard, for his brother. In fact, he pretended that one old grave that no longer showed a name or a date was his brother's. That stone had been placed flatly into the ground, and its edges were now soft and deep in the moss and grass. Malcolm had taken to speaking to it. "At school they feel bad for me but they are afraid to talk to me," he said. "I would say they like me a little more but a little less since you died." And once, quietly, "Mother seems to have gone a bit mad." Today Malcolm told Karl of the letters from Jennifer, all of which his mother had now given him. But Malcolm didn't say what he really wanted to say: *Tell me now that you left this earth before your baby was deposited into the boathouse. Tell me that had you lived, she would not have been in a canoe on the cold fall water.* Malcolm didn't say that. But he wouldn't write back to Jennifer, either. What she had done, no. Malcolm would have no part of her.

From the edge of the woods he tore off three branches that had given birth to bright red berries. He surrounded them with gone-by golden ferns, a sort of bouquet, and he placed it atop the grave.

Passing Clara and Paul's, Malcolm decided to stop in and see if they didn't need anything. From the front step he could hear the baby wailing. He knocked and knocked and when no one came he opened the door and stuck his head in.

Paul held screaming Alice in his arms. Malcolm had never heard her cry so hard.

"It's not a good time for a visit," Paul told him, but Malcolm didn't budge. "Malcolm," Paul snapped. "Shut the door and be gone."

Where was Clara? "Higher," Malcolm said through Alice's wails.

"Excuse me?"

Malcolm pushed the door wider and walked right in, his arms held out for the baby. Paul backed up and told him again to leave, but Malcolm kept reaching for the child, and when Alice's cries got so loud and so fierce that Malcolm worried she would choke, finally he shouted, "For God's sake, lift her higher over your shoulder!"

"Out," Paul said steadily. "You get out of this house."

Malcolm had tears now, too.

"Don't you ever come here again," Paul said. He put his hand on Malcolm's shoulder and began to shove him toward the door.

Malcolm didn't fight back, but he did yell as he was pushed through the house. The words came out quickly and repeatedly, and it wasn't until he was back in the fall air that he realized just what he was saying, and how awful it was. "That baby belongs to me, that is my brother's baby, that baby belongs to me, that is my brother's baby," over and over again.

"Never come back," Paul said.

The door shut and the secret was out and Malcolm looked up to the sky and thought, Dear God, help my mother, for the indecency is upon us.

In town Malcolm was standing at the grocery store with his hand wrapped around the doorknob, unsure if he was ready to see anyone, when he heard his name called.

"Father," he said desperately, for it had sounded like him, and Otto's store was right next door, and how Malcolm had wanted to go in there and sit down and be loved, but he had been ashamed of his own tears. Now, thankfully, here his father was.

"Malcolm," the man repeated. Malcolm looked up and his

face reddened. Not his father at all. Still, this man placed a hand upon the boy's head and gave his hair a tousle. In his adulthood Malcolm would realize that at that time, the man could not have been much more than twenty years old, but now, standing on Main Street in the fall wind, Malcolm believed the man to be weathered with age, and wise. Mike Shaw, his father's boathouse tenant.

"I heard you like babies."

"Sorry?"

"Babies?"

Malcolm shrugged.

"Clara Thorton. She says you got a way with the little shits."

"I've got to get a turkey for my mother."

"Woods got turkeys," the man said.

"Yes. There's a whole family of them at my house. Thirty, my mother watches and keeps track."

"You wants a turkey you shoots a turkey," the man said. Slowly he removed a bag of tobacco from his back pocket and opened its flap. Inside he already had a few cigarettes rolled. He took one out and put it to his lips. Then the man turned and unbuttoned his top button and lifted the loose slack of his shirt to his face to block the wind and in one try, using only one hand, he lit the match to light the cigarette. Even to Malcolm there was something attractive in these easy movements.

"Turkey got your tongue?" Mike Shaw asked. The cigarettes were without a filter and on the tip of his own tongue there lay a shred of tobacco. He pursed his lips and pointed his tongue and gave a little blow and that took care of it. "Old enough to smoke?" he asked the boy.

"I've got to get my mother a turkey."

"Ain't nothing a woman likes more than fresh hunted meat, believe you me. Come over, why don't you."

"I couldn't."

"I've got a baby and I need your help. My woman's in a mood and it's aimed straight at me. Heard you're the one to look for, so come over. I'll teach you how to get yourself a turkey."

"I'd like to buy my turkey."

"Go ahead in there then. I'll wait right here. Tell you now they don't got one, you got to order them ahead, don't you know that? Your mother knows that. Go in and come back out and then we'll see if you trust me."

Malcolm went in. He looked in the freezer and he kept looking and finally Mr. Potter asked if he couldn't help and Malcolm found out that Mike Shaw was right, you've got to order them ahead.

"What else goes in a Thanksgiving dinner?" he asked Mr. Potter.

"Potato, squash, don't your mother grow that?"

"My mother keeps flowers mostly."

"You know what a lady likes? Cornstalks, a little decoration. I got a barrel of them a dime a piece but I'll give you two for free."

"All right," Malcolm said. He left the store with one big squash and two cornstalks and outside Mike Shaw told him that it did not look like his Thanksgiving dinner would turn out to be much, which made Malcolm want to sob right there on the street.

They rode silently in Mike Shaw's truck. It was only a minute or two anyway. When they pulled up in front of the boathouse Mike leaned over and opened the glove box and took out a map and told Malcolm to go up and meet the missus, but Malcolm just sat there. Mike Shaw got out and unfolded the map and spread it upon the hood of the truck. The woman came out onto the high porch then, and from the way she stood with her hand placed gently at the base of her stomach, Malcolm felt sure that she was pregnant again.

"Go on," Mike Shaw said, and pointed his chin quickly upward, toward the porch, then let it fall slowly back into place. To Malcolm that was such a sure and firm motion, and in the coming weeks he would practice it in front of the mirror.

"I don't remember her name."

"She don't know what's right for a man, Malcolm. Go on up and fix her. Take the baby. Make her smile." He set the map on the dirt driveway and placed a rock over it so it wouldn't blow away, and then he punched the hood of the truck to make it open. "June," he said. "June's her name."

When Malcolm approached the staircase she had already gone inside and the baby had begun to cry. He hadn't spoken with these tenants before and his father had told him expressly not to. At the door Malcolm stood for some time, and when he looked down to Mike Shaw, the man pointed his chin again to say to just go in. Malcolm pushed the door open and called softly, "Sorry."

"Well come in or come out," the woman said.

The room was a flood of yellow—yellow linoleum floor and yellow countertops and one yellow metal table with two yellow metal chairs. The color was broken only by one wall lined with skis and trophies and medals. Malcolm stood in the doorway and gazed toward that wall. Karl had been a skier. He would have liked to know that the man who rented out their father's boathouse apartment was the very same man who won every single race at the ski area.

The woman cleared her throat and Malcolm looked at her. "Sorry," he said again.

"Shut the door behind you."

"I'm Malcolm," he said.

"I know who you are."

Suddenly the baby wailed. There was an old, worn curtain patterned with cartoon racecars that hung from a doorway off the big room, and Malcolm could tell the boy was in there. The woman's face was so red and so taut that he could see her veins.

"May I?" he dared. He was already across the room, had already lifted the curtain. Now he put his hands on that body, and there, Malcolm felt good once more. The life and sweetness of it filled him right up. He pulled the baby to his shoulder, and didn't this one smell just like his brother's? Yes, this one was just as good. There now, yes. You're okay.

"Tea?" the woman said.

Malcolm shook his head.

"Coffee?"

"No thank you."

"Well sit down why don't you."

With the baby in his arms Malcolm sat down at the table. This was the first apartment he had ever been in. It was in a cove—there was no vision of the open water from here—but still the view lifted Malcolm up in some real way. The front of the building was lined with windows and if Malcolm were to walk out of them he would fall and land straight in the water.

"He's not even my husband," the woman said as she handed Malcolm a bottle. "People in this town think we're married but he wouldn't have me. Do you think that's terrible?"

"There," Malcolm said, and rubbed at the baby's cheek. "There now."

Mike heard that. He had come up the stairs and now he came fully into the room. His footsteps made the floor tremble. "So you've got a way with the shits," he said. "June ain't got that."

June rose and Mike Shaw took her seat and spread his legs and untucked his shirt. "She's got another bun in the oven and she'll need your help, June will." June was at the window now, looking out to the lake. "A deal," Mike Shaw said. "Malcolm, let's us men talk outside."

The deal was that Malcolm would come in and check on June each day after school while Mike Shaw went out west to make a real go at being a ski racer. Malcolm was to play a game with June, see that the baby, Todd, quieted and she had her rest. See that she didn't get into any funny business.

"Do you know what that means?"

"Indecency with a man," Malcolm said quickly.

Mike Shaw hooted at that, and gave Malcolm's back a tap so hard that the boy keeled forward. When he came back to, Mike Shaw said, "Out west, Malcolm. Open road, open land. A man needs his freedom, you understand. You like babies now but you'll be a man one day."

Malcolm said yes and asked only, "How long?"

Mike Shaw said, "Nope."

That gave Malcolm courage. Or a kind of anger that he had not felt before and that certainly disguised itself as courage. He asked how Mike Shaw would hold up his end of the deal.

Mike Shaw clapped his hands together and gave a little laugh, and then, seeing the boy was serious, he said, "Anything you like."

To care for his mother, to be a man, that is what Malcolm would like. He said, "A gun. I would like a gun and I would like to learn how to shoot it."

"Well then," Mike Shaw said.

They shot off the dock, with Malcolm saying a silent apology and prayer about the noise and the danger of it. It was a rifle and the first shot made him buckle back and fall into Mike Shaw's firm body and Mike Shaw said, "There we go. Now you can protect my woman." Next shot he told Malcolm to kneel down so he didn't fall again.

"I am not a child," Malcolm said, and he shot the gun and did not waver and next he said, "I would like to take it home with me."

"Your gun," Mike Shaw said.

"You cannot expect me to carry a gun through town." Where had his bravery come from? Malcolm could feel it, a slow boil in his chest.

"Well then," Mike Shaw said, his voice lofty, a way to put an end to the child's demands. Still, he went to his truck and found the boy a duffel bag, which fit nearly the whole gun into it, along with the squash and cornstalks. It would do.

"Look," June said when they returned inside. She was at the window and Malcolm went to her just as a loon made its dive under. "Guess where it will come up," she said.

Malcolm pointed and together they counted and in forty-eight seconds the loon rose just where he had said it would. Mike Shaw tapped the boy on the back and the boy slung the bag over his shoulder and it was the last Malcolm would see of him for years and years to come.

In his mind, things had been much different. Perhaps the turkeys will emerge sometime before Thanksgiving, he thought once, but the thought was fleeting. Mostly Malcolm thought that sometime in the future he could learn to hunt. First he would put the gun in the woodshed, where Sophie would not find it. Slowly Malcolm would grow accustomed to the weapon. He would carry it in the woods. The Randolph boys, they must know how to hunt, and Malcolm rather quickly imagined asking those boys to teach him. With this skill, oh, how he could impress his father. Perhaps even teach his father. Shooting a turkey for this holiday was not something Malcolm had expected to do.

The lane of old maples stopped just as the hill crested and the land spread open and the two houses—Malcolm's own and the Randolphs'—came into view. The Randolphs' house lay to the west and Malcolm's tall white colonial just twenty steps above. To stop and simply watch the sweep of the land—Malcolm was not accustomed to that, but now he did it and it felt the sort of thing a man would do. Standing in that way he decided that his house was beautiful, strong and solid, and that it looked like it had come from the time of the revolution. Instinctively he began to march his feet. Inside he hummed. The wind swept from the north, up through the lane of trees. Malcolm turned. There the biggest of all the turkeys stood perched on the stone wall. The gun was loaded. Without thought or complication Malcolm took the gun from the bag, aimed, and shot. The turkey's chest rose outward like a balloon and then sank in a series of convulsions. The flutter of her family behind her was loud and quick. Now, alone, that great big turkey lay. From where he stood he could see a small red stream emerge. Was it a leaf? Yes, surely a red maple leaf. No blood, not even a trickle, Malcolm told himself. I did not shoot that animal. But already Malcolm could sense that never again would those turkeys return. Slowly he put the gun back in the duffel. He walked to the dead being and picked it up by its neck, then brought it in close to his body. It was warm against his chest and for a moment he believed he could call it back to life. "Forgive me," he whispered. He put his nose into the animal. It smelled of deep, untouched forest. He held his breath so as not to cry. As he walked toward his house, Mrs. Randolph stood and moved her head in a slow, womanly way. It was not a message of approval.

Sophie was inside, at the kitchen sink, that old cookbook Hjalmar had given her all those years ago open beside her. She had meant to choose something to cook for her son but had gotten caught up watching those turkeys instead. When the largest fell, Sophie squeezed the glass in her hand until it splintered into pieces.

"Mother," Malcolm said when he found her. He had left the dead turkey in the woodshed. He had forfeited his own wool jacket for the bird, wrapped her up in it and placed her on top of the woodpile. Now his mother's own blood painted the dishwater that filled the sink. He reached for her hand but she pulled it back. It was clear that a piece of glass was lodged deep in her finger. "Mother," Malcolm said again. "We've got to get you to the doctor."

"Call Signe," Sophie said. Once more when he reached for her she flinched. "Don't you come near me. Call Aunt Signe and don't you ever come near me."


In the years to come, Sophie would look at that clean, precise scar that ran the length of the pointer finger on her left hand and she would recall the words that she had said to her son. With the turkeys gone (because they did disappear, every last one of them, forever) Sophie wandered from room to room and eventually in her steps she turned that anger at her son inward; how terrible she had been. Had she been so terrible to Karl? She took the letter opener from Otto's desk and ran it down the length of the box that sat on her hope chest, beneath a pile of fresh towels. The name split in half, KARL OT on one flap and TO WICKHOLM on the other. Carefully Sophie untwisted the top of the plastic bag and plunged her hand into the remains of her son. Like sand she let him fall through her fingers. She took up only one handful and placed it in a tin. Her finger still had its stitches, six of them, and she had already removed the bandage, so Karl's ashes stuck to that moist line of cut. She did not wash them away.

Sophie had not said as much, but the Swedish church in Boston that her aunt Signe used to take her to was the place where she had first come to God. She would like to take her son there. She placed the tin with her son's ashes in her purse, along with a train schedule, and first thing Sunday morning Sophie tiptoed across the hall and opened Malcolm's door and called his name to tell him she would take him on an adventure, they would go to Boston and they could go to lunch there and he could get a box of chocolates and they could even go visit that old Chinese street he liked, she would give him five dollars and he could spend it any old way.

"Malcolm?" she said. The harsh wind knocked at the storm windows. "Malcolm, honey, wake up. Malcolm?" She rushed across the room and tore off the covers though she knew already that her son was gone.

Jennifer in Oregon. That was Sophie's first thought as she flung open his top drawer and reached in the back to just the place where she herself would hide something. There they were, those three opened letters. Like a beast she tore through them. Then she went to the window and threw it open. The lake rose up below and Sophie screamed her son's name, knowing he would not hear.

"Over here, honey," Mrs. Randolph had told Malcolm the day before. Winter was soon and she and her boys had begun to keep a fire in the old woodstove on the porch. From her rocking chair she could reach both the pile of old clapboards and the top of the stove, so she did not have to get up to keep the fire fed.

Malcolm had the dead turkey in his arms. When he had pulled it by its feet from the top of the woodpile and brought it down, its wings had given a flap and he had thought it would take life and flight again, but of course it would not.

"Boys," Mrs. Randolph had called quietly, and that was all. They came out and they knew just what was to be done. When he was shown and it was his turn with the feathers Malcolm took Mrs. Randolph's seat. It was warm and safe and each time he pulled a feather that pink skin gave a little tug and then bounced back down.

"If you ain't going to eat it," Mrs. Randolph had said, "I'm guessing there's a woman with a baby and another on the way wouldn't mind a gift from you."

So that is what Malcolm had done. His family would eat beef that his father had bought last spring from the Phillipses' farm. Otto thought that family to be good, hard workers, so he had bought the meat despite the fact that he considered himself a modern man who ought to buy meat at the store. The Wickholms would eat beef on Thanksgiving, and June would have a turkey.

And the gun would go in the lake. Malcolm had decided that as he sat there on that porch and looked down toward the cold water. The lake would be frozen soon. He would go out tomorrow.


June said she would cook the turkey early because it gave her an excuse to turn the oven on and heat the place up. If she had seen Malcolm go out in his canoe she would have said that he had better not go in this weather. Malcolm paddled out to the center of the open water. In the distance Kettleborough sat small as a village for gnomes. He laid his paddle on the floor of the canoe and took up the gun. He held it high above his head and counted to ten. With the wind he could scarcely hold his arms steady. When he released the gun, it fell more slowly than he would have thought possible. In the water it spun downward, and he watched it go. When it was out of sight he took up his paddle and though the lake was rough he did not have fear, for somewhere deep within Malcolm knew he would never die in this big lake.

Sophie left the window open and ran to the telephone to call Otto at work.

"Our Malcolm has left us," she said when he answered. Her voice was quiet but firm, with a pronounced shake to it. She had to grip one hand on the banister to keep from tipping over. "It's our fault," she said bravely.

Otto did not speak, but she could hear his slow, steady breath on the other end of the line.

"Ours," she said again. She didn't care if Mrs. Randolph heard. "The baby," she said. "You and I," she said. She would have gone on, but Otto cut her off.

"One more word," he said slowly, "and I will put down this telephone and not ever speak to you again."

Sophie opened her mouth but no sound emerged. She dropped the phone, let it hang there by its cord, and stood alone in the bright living room. After a few breaths she crossed the room, found her purse, and ran out the door.

Mrs. Randolph had heard Sophie calling for her son, and now she could see that Malcolm was at the bottom of the hill, headed homeward, a baby in his arms. So we've finally come to this, she thought. She looked toward the Wickholm house just in time to see Sophie run out the door, slip on the ice, and fall to the ground.

"He's here," Mrs. Randolph hollered as she rushed the short distance from her own porch to Sophie's house. "Malcolm. He's coming up the hill."

The contents of Sophie's purse had spilled in her fall. A small can of aerosol hair spray and a fold of powder. There, three pictures of her illegitimate grandbaby. Her wallet, a tin, a letter addressed to Jennifer in Oregon. When Mrs. Randolph arrived at Sophie's side, heaving, out of breath, she picked up Sophie's spilled belongings and placed them back inside the purse. All except those photos. These she handed over one by one. Sophie took them in her hand and looked up at the figure that hovered above her. The sun was bright and large behind Mrs. Randolph, and because of it her face wasn't a face at all, but just a shadow of a being. Still, Sophie knew it was her neighbor. The two had never even shaken hands before. What had Sophie become? She gave Mrs. Randolph her empty hand, and though just moments ago Sophie had meant to flee Otto and Kettleborough and the entire life she had created, now she looked back toward her tall house.

"We're not all perfect, is we?" Mrs. Randolph said, and helped to pull Sophie to her feet.

With the ice on the ground, Otto had driven down to the shop rather than walk, and now when he pulled in Mrs. Randolph was back on her porch, and Sophie and Malcolm were standing in front of their own house. Otto could see before he even pulled the car to a stop that Malcolm held a sleeping baby in his arms.

"It's not Karl's," Malcolm called as his father emerged from the car. His voice was loud, a fight against the harsh wind. Otto walked to them, stood before them with his arms crossed at his chest. He looked at his wife and then let his eyes fall on his son. Malcolm clenched his teeth. His father had never hit him but he had a clear vision now of that firm hand coming across his face. Yet the hand did not, and with no one else speaking Malcolm continued. "This is Todd. June's son. June who lives at the boathouse. I have offered to help her. She is alone. She said I could bring the baby up to meet Mother."

"June has a husband."

"He is gone out west," Malcolm said, and handed the baby to Sophie. She took him willingly as she stood there in the life she knew she would never have the courage to leave. "He is not—" Malcolm began, but his father cut him off. What would he have said? He is not a replacement for our Karl's child?

"Hush," Otto said. "That's enough. We'll be quiet now. That's quite enough."

And it wasn't enough, but in another way it was. They were quiet. People can live that way.

# Free

## 1959

TWO YEARS AFTER they married, Clara Thorton told her husband, Paul, that she wanted to drive as far east as they could get.
He had finished a job and had a hunk of money and that was the
way he preferred to live—build a house, take a break until the
money ran out. Together they outfitted the van. They secured a
crib to the backside of the driver's seat. They put a bed where the
backseats belonged and she sewed curtains and he even made
little wooden cupboards for her things. There was a camp stove
and rope and tarp to extend their living space, and they were in
love then, and things would be good.

Before they had adopted Alice, Clara had been different; of

course she had. She had liked to disappear at night, to go off alone and watch the stars if they were out, or the moon, and if neither was possible then to just look into the warm houses and imagine the lives inside. She never told him where she went at these times and he understood to not worry or ask. She liked to drink wine then, too, and often when he kissed her maroon lips they would be sweet and pruned. They hadn't expected to keep the baby for good but they hadn't worried over it, at least not together. He had said that it would be a fun project—those words exactly—and so she had agreed.

Her worry took over when the papers were signed and the baby was theirs and the promise was made to not ever tell the child where it was she had come from. "Is she breathing?" Clara would ask. "Paul, Paul, wake up, she feels hot, is she dying?"

"Ease up," had become his constant refrain, and in protest to her nervousness he had become careless. He let the baby cry for longer than his heart would have allowed. He put a bite of squash into her mouth in the days before she was supposed to eat solids.

But on this trip they drove over the mountains and when they crossed into Canada the land spread open and she opened the window and hung her head out to let her long hair trail behind her. She felt free as she ever had. They shared a few beers as they drove and they kept their hands on each other's lap and the baby stayed silent, she usually did, and they together laughed.

And look at those cliffs! Some red as a desert and others slick and black, all of them dropping straight down to that endless blue ocean. They didn't take their time getting to the cliff that was nearly one thousand miles from Kettleborough, all the way on a northeastern leg of the continent, only a throw from New-foundland, where they planned to park the van and spend a week. They just drove for nearly twelve hours, parked on a logging road and slept, and drove for twelve more hours. Clara keeps a photograph from that night on the logging road. The roadside was filled with knapweed, lupine, and Queen Anne's lace. Paul balanced a steak on two sticks and cooked it over the fire. The baby was calm, and both Paul and Clara felt filled up with all they would ever need. The sun stayed late, and the photograph is dim, but there Paul is, up close, looking at the camera and giving for the last time that perfectly mischievous smile that she knew was reserved for her alone.

The place they were headed to was a cove at least one hundred miles from any real feeling of civilization. The last leg of the journey—perhaps forty miles—took nearly three hours. It was that washboard dirt road, and the height. Out there the only place for living was atop the cliffs, so that's where the road ran, right along the edge, and death became not a presence or an event but a place, just there, one step to the east.

"Ease up," Paul said once as he drove, because Clara wanted him to slow down even more.

The road ended at a village of trailers and weak houses trapped on one side by ocean and the other by deep, wet forest. At the tip of the village—which was the tip of the land—there lay a field of grass dotted by picnic tables. This was the campground where they would stay. It was the only accommodation in the village. There was an outhouse and a water pump and a shower that they could feed dimes into. Paul chose their spot and Clara told him that she wanted one farther from the edge and again he said it, "Ease up," so she did. The bells on the buoys clanged with the easy motion of the water, and this was as beautiful a place as Clara had ever been to.

.   .   .

They ate lobster bought from the man who ran the campground. He had a strong accent born of this far-off place, and they did not understand everything he said, but Clara knew he said that whales lived out there in the cove, and that if she watched long enough she would surely see them. After the baby was asleep she lay down for a time with Paul, but when the moon rose she went back outside and sat on the grass with her heels touching the edge of the cliff, and she did not take her eyes off the gleaming water for hours. A ship went by, and though it was probably only a ferry on its way to Newfoundland, Clara imagined red carpets and a brass band, women in billowing dresses headed to a foreign land. Eventually she fell asleep out there. Paul woke her in the early hours of morning and she sat up wide-eyed, happy. There was a mass of birds above, Paul had been watching them for about an hour while Clara slept on the grass, and they circled and dove and circled and dove. They were terns; Paul knew their name. They would float on their cloud of air as if nothing in the world would disturb them, ever, and then one bird would decide to drop and bam, the bird was gone. Bam, bam, one after another, that is the only way to describe it. The birds dove down to the water and right through the surface with the force of a bullet.

"Feeding grounds," Paul said, and he told Clara there would be whales there. Which there were; he saw many of them. "There!" he would say, and point, and "There!" again, but not once did Clara see a whale he pointed to.

The cliff was broad, but in one spot near to them it transformed into a narrow, rocky bridge like the neck of an hourglass. Over that short bridge you could walk to a small splatter of grassy land that seemed itself the very end of the earth. After breakfast Paul draped the baby over his shoulder and headed toward that spot.

Clara called to him, told him not to cross with Alice. And he heard her, plain as day he did. But he did not respond.

They had been up for a few hours, Clara had hardly slept, and by now a cranky weariness had set in. "God damn it," she said, but he crossed without trouble, of course he would, and Clara went to the van. There she saw that he had left the gas to the camp stove on. He could have blown up their entire van. Had the baby been in it he could have killed her. In a rage Clara crossed that land bridge. She tripped at the edge, and had she not been able to catch her balance she would have tumbled to her death. Paul did not see it, for his eyes were pinned decidedly upon the water.

"Give her to me," she said. He patted the baby's back and kissed her head. "You're a child," Clara told her husband. It was the way he had ignored her. He did this when he believed he was right; he had an uncanny ability to act as though she were only a space of air that he could see right through. "I'm tired of being married to a child," she said. She held her arms out and eventually he handed the baby her way without looking at his wife. As she headed toward that small land bridge with the baby in her arms, she wished wildly that she had not said what she had said. She did not like heights, and she wanted Paul there with her now to hold her hand and make her know that she was safe. She wanted him to carry the baby across because she did not believe that she herself was capable. She should have laughed and apologized. Yet he was still watching that great ocean and Clara did not admit her error. With her baby in her arms she headed back for the narrow strip of land.

Later in her life Clara will think for a time that she could become a marine biologist. She will hear a young woman speak on the radio about a moment out on the ocean in the middle of the night when she and her colleagues discovered that dolphins feed in groups. No one had known this yet and there they were, awake, watching it take place. The vastness of the night and the stars and the ocean, and the singularity of those dolphins and herself, and the moment when they all converge—Clara will know just what that woman must have felt. But for Clara, it will turn out, sitting on the cliff and watching a whale rise is enough.

She made it back to their camp spot just fine, and by the time Paul came back to her, the baby had eaten and was sleeping in her crib in the van and Clara thought that the fight would be over, that together they could walk the one path that led up the road and then down the hill to the base of the cliff. There was a small beach there; they could find driftwood and whalebones, sea glass to line their kitchen windows. But Paul was silent, and this alone sent Clara back into her rage. She went to the glove box—what was she looking for?—and he went to the driver's seat, where he had left his backpack. He began to root through it with abandon, and Clara asked him to please quiet down, the baby was sleeping. This made him rustle his things more loudly. She asked him once more to quiet down and this time he cursed her. Clara was perched halfway in the van now, one leg up on the ledge to climb into the seat. The terns were gone and the sun was high and the water behind her glistened with life and light. She reached her arm over the emergency brake and grabbed hold of her husband's bag. She pulled at it but he would not let go. Eventually his hand grabbed hold of her arm—not on purpose, she would decide and believe with her whole heart—and the pressure of it hurt fiercely.

"Damn you," she said, and let go of the backpack.

They were both out of the van, standing by the campfire ring where they had shared such a glorious night less than twenty-four hours before, and she knew exactly how to end the fight and move on to being good again, all she needed to do was claim fault, every last bit of it, and she was about to do just that when they heard that faint creak. They both turned around swiftly, but the van was already moving. For the rest of her life, Clara will be sure that for Paul, at that moment everything else in the world was absolutely still. Only that van with his baby inside existed, and only that van moved, slowly. It didn't have far to go before it lumbered over the cliff. When it fell it was with a certain peace, even grace. There was no tumbling involved. Just like a tern that van went straight for the water.

But for Clara, more than the van existed at that moment. Paul was already running toward the path to the beach, but when Clara looked up she saw it, that slick black back of a whale. Upward it rose, slowly and smoothly as though it were a hand attached to the underwater clock that made the world itself move on. Clara watched it fall back in and rise again. Over and over again that whale rose and fell and how could she ever explain to Paul that it was for that vision that she did not move? That she had known he was headed toward the beach but she had also believed that what had happened had happened, but that here was her chance alone to watch a great old being rise from the depths of the earth?

He screamed her name as he went. He needed her help. He was a large, strong man, but they both knew that she was the stronger swimmer. She did run to help him, but by the time she got to the beach he was already in the water. She did not go in after him. She had no faith that anything could be done. For even then, just minutes after it had happened, it seemed clear to her: a whale had entered this cruel and beautiful world at the precise time that her infant had exited it. It was not a belief that would quell the sorrow but it was a belief that might add some order to the mystery.

Underwater, the van wasn't hard to find. Like a puzzle piece it had fit itself in between two boulders. Its nose faced upward and its tail end rested upon the sandy ocean floor. Paul found it quickly. The tide was coming in but he must have felt stronger than the force of the entire ocean. The windows were up and the doors were shut. Clara could imagine his time under that water. She could see seaweed long and thick as trees in a rainforest, and she could see that van lit up, glowing with the life of her daughter inside. She could see her Paul taking one breath to inspect his options, and then one more to dive under and rescue the baby. She could see him as an adept explorer in the cold ocean. But none of that could possibly be true. Aside from the terror, it must have been dark and it must have been sheer luck that led his hand to the door of the van, and led him to the crib where his baby lay, her back against the bars, grasping desperately upward.

She was okay. Miraculously she was. He came up with her in his arms and he tapped her back. Her skin had turned a little blue but she coughed and she did not cry but she did breathe; she breathed fine then and she still does today. It must have been five minutes that she was under the water. They would never know. It could have been less and it could have been more but anyway Clara's husband had the baby in his arms and he walked right past Clara on the beach. The few other people in that cove were on the beach now, too, though neither Clara nor Paul realized it. Paul walked up the hill to the shack where the owner of the campground stayed, but he wasn't there so he walked to the man's truck and started it. Clara got in and for nearly six hours they rode in silence to the nearest hospital. Paul would not hand the baby over. He had wrapped her in Clara's sweater and now he kept her on his lap, and stopped every half hour or so to hold her against his chest. How Clara would have liked to be held like that. But she knew then that never again would her Paul come back to her. Her fault this time had been too great.

# PART TWO

# Crossing

## 1971 & 1994

I WAS WITH my father when I first crossed the bridge to King's Point. I was twelve and we were to attend a party of some distant relatives whom I had never met before. Up we went to the peak of the bridge, and for a moment all earth was shielded from us, nothing remaining but endless sky and lake. Right then I imagined a body launching itself over the edge and going onward, unleashed from this weighted life. But the truck crested the hill and we descended.

King's Point is just a mile from the Kettleborough Pier, and beneath the bridge a narrow strip of rocks connects it to mainland. But more often than not, those rocks are covered with water, so in truth King's is more of an island than a point. I had heard that famous people lived out there, actors and politicians. Their houses dotted the edge, while the center of the point remained a mass of thick pine. There was—and still is—only one road, which circled the perimeter and dropped sharply to the mansions and lake. Each mansion was numbered and the house we were headed for was 24. It wasn't hard to locate—its mailbox was roughly the size of my own closet. The house itself was not visible from the road, but when the car dropped down the drive that grand white house rose up as though straight out of the water. It was the stuff of movies, with white pillars on the porch and stone statues in the yard, laughter rolling off the granite floors and into the lush green grass.

My father climbed out of the truck and walked right to the door and opened it up and went in as though he had been in a place like this a thousand times before. I clung at his back. We entered a drawing room that our own house could fit into. There were maybe twenty people in there. From that wide, echo-filled room three stairs rose to an open kitchen. All of this was granite, save for the three-basin sink, which was metal. The adults clanked their glasses and tossed back their heads, and it wasn't long until my father joined right in, though it was clear even to my childhood self that he was of another breed entirely.

"Don't you look like Paul Newman," one woman said to him.

"Aren't you a bowl of chocolate chips."

"Don't you look like Robert Redford." Devnet's mother said that.

Devnet is where the story begins. I was promptly introduced to her, as she and her younger brother, Thomas, were the only other children there. They were staying at this house—owned by their grandparents—for the entire summer.

"Preteen," Devnet called me after our introduction. She was thirteen and as she told me this she sighed and put an exasper-

ated hand to her forehead and said, "Oh, Alice, it's all about to
start happening to you. Love, ache, lies, the works." The way she
said that word, *ache,* it did indeed sound just barely out of my
reach. *Devnet,* too, the name itself. It sounded womanly and I
asked her where it came from.

"I'm named after my parents' dead baby," she told me. Then
she moved behind me, boldly grabbed my waist, and steered
me to her bedroom. There were bunk beds there, and Devnet
climbed up to the top and instructed me to join her. Her brother,
when he appeared, was ordered to remain on the floor.

"Today we saw the monster of the lake," he called to me.

"Hush up," Devnet said. She crossed her legs, asked me what I
liked to do, and listlessly spoke of the woes of teenage life.

"First we saw the shadow and then it flighted away," Thomas
said.

I told Devnet that I liked to ski. She scoffed at this, and once
again reminded me that it was all about to start happening. And
then to her brother, "Scat," she said, "skedaddle." He did, and
Devnet went on with her lecture, though I was much more interested in the monster, who had the reputation of appearing just
before trouble.

"The gnomes are coming, Alice!" Thomas called from the
hallway. "The giants are coming!"

"I'm thirteen and already life has become *too much,*" Devnet
said. She lay back against the pillow with one arm thrown lan-
guidly upward. I said I had to use the bathroom—a fib—and
climbed off that bed. I let Thomas lead me to my next adventure, which he discovered when he opened the refrigerator door.
There were lobsters in there, at least twenty of the faintly blue
beasts. When we moved those thick plastic bags of them to the
counter it wasn't but a minute before every single lobster began
violently to thrash for life.

"We've got to save them," Thomas said with conviction. Panicked, I plugged up the metal sink and filled it with cold water. Thomas reached over and dumped an entire canister of salt in. In a soft and urgent voice he spoke to them, said, "There now, you little cloppers. Now we'll get you to the ocean, there, now you can swim free."

"If it weren't for the rest of the world I would not eat you," I whispered as those sad, maroon beings began to slow their hold on life. "I've got to fit in, don't I?"

Devnet found me quickly enough. She pulled me away from the sink, saying that her father wanted us to run to the store with him. And what would have happened, had I not done that?

"He says my stupid mother forgot the corn," she said.

I had no mother, and wanted one desperately, so I was shocked to hear Devnet speak of her own mother in such a way. She pushed me out the door. Dusk had just begun to fall. Devnet's father was already in the driver's seat. I had not told my father I was going but I got in without protest. On the way to the store, her father had her take the wheel so he could remove his jacket, and once that was off he tipped his seat back a bit and told her to keep steering us the whole way there. This frightened me, and I sat straight-backed in the seat, preparing my arms and legs for the event of a crash, laboring over whether or not to speak up for my own safety. But we made it to the store just fine, and Devnet's father sent her in with a twenty-dollar bill. That stretch of time when he and I sat silent in the car together, what an assaulting fear it filled me with. His breath was slow and heavy, and now and then his eyes—which were dark and lovely; he was a remarkably attractive man—would catch me in the rearview mirror and just hold me there. I had a strange sense that he would start the car and drive me away, take me as his unwilling lover. Finally Devnet reappeared. She was wearing blue-jean cutoff shorts with a bathing suit underneath—I don't know why I hadn't noticed this before or why I noticed it now. But I did, and as she walked across the pavement to the black car with that large bag of corn, she just looked so skinny and helpless that for a moment I became certain in a very unchildlike way that I would fare better than she in this short life. She thrust the corn into the backseat. She was allowed to steer again on the way back to the mansion, and this time I wasn't afraid, though I should have been.

As we turned from mainland to cross over, I caught sight of a man walking onto the bridge, heading our way. Then I looked toward the lake just as a red-tailed hawk, wings expanded, dove from a tree to float on a wave of sky. Only when the car thumped and I plunged forward against the back of the driver's seat did I lose sight of that hawk. We had hit it, I thought suddenly. But then I looked out the window to see that instead of a hawk, the body of the man we had hit flew over the edge of the bridge. How he soared, suspended on an invisible ledge of air. When he dropped it was sudden—that air just let go. He hit the water and, seamlessly as a maple's leaves turning, the lake transformed to a pool of red around him.

Devnet began to scream, though it seemed not out of horror but out of incredulousness. "That man jumped in front of us," she said a few times. "That man jumped in front of us!" Then her statement matured.

"That man just committed suicide!" As she repeated this her head darted back and forth—she seemed to think there was a crowd of people about her, all waiting for an explanation.

"But—" I began, quietly, but Devnet spun around in her seat.

"Shut up," she said. She reached for my collar and grabbed hold, clenching her teeth. "You're the one who's not even really a part of our family, so you just shut up. I know where you really come from. You just shut up."

We were entirely righted on the bridge, just at the crest, so that all we could see ahead was that great expanse of dim purple sky, another world entirely. I didn't know what she meant. Her words just entered me, steady and vacant. Within a week they would make a home. For now I simply noticed how well dressed Devnet's father was. He took up the linen blazer, which earlier he had removed, and from his pocket withdrew a flask.

"Drink," he said, and turned in his seat to face me. I did, one gulp. It was brandy, and to this day even the scent turns me nauseous.

"Don't you say a word," he said. He was remarkably serene. He had done this many times, it seemed that way. "This will calm you down," he said, meaning the liquor. "You say a word it's jail for all of us." That calm voice, he could have been suggesting what we might have for dinner or what game we might play.

"That man committed suicide!" Devnet screamed again.

"It's true," her father said to her. Then he turned to me. "If you open your fat mouth," he said, "then you and your father will be dead."

"That's true, too," Devnet said. "I seen him kill before, my father's serious."

He whipped around then and smacked Devnet hard across the face. Her hand went to where he had hit, but she didn't so much as shudder.

Why didn't I jump out of the car, swim to that floating man? He could have been alive. I knew how to swim. I couldn't have saved him but surely to try would have said something about my character.

By now that man, George Collins, twenty years old, had disappeared. But he would be found soon enough, caught in the twisted roots of the large pine that reached over the bank, into the water. It was the same tree that hawk had soared from, and it still stands today. Devnet's father eased us down the bridge and pulled off to the side. He handed Devnet his flask and a full bottle that he pulled from beneath his seat, and told her to empty them both in the lake, fill them with water, and come dump them over the front of the car.

"Anyone drives by while you're down there, you jump right in the lake. Car comes while you're up here, you pour that water over your head and make a show of cooling off."

Devnet seemed sickeningly pleased with her role. As I sat in the back and let her father continue his slow, firm threats, one hand holding so tight to my thigh that I had blotches of yellow and purple skin for months to come, I watched Devnet complete her task with efficiency.

By the time we got back to the house it seemed that Devnet and her father had already forgotten. They hulled the corn together and put it on to steam, an exemplary father-daughter pair. My father stood in the corner, sipping on a beer. I went to him, stood at his side. Had he thought to ask me if I was all right, how the drive went, any such thing, I would have fallen open. As it was he said nothing and shortly we were in line for our lobsters. I was last in line, and by the time my plate was made everyone else was seated at the dining table, which was in that large room that was open to the kitchen but three steps down. At the top of the steps I stood, quivering, that poor dead bug on my plate. As I inched forward to take my first step, the lobster slid off and dropped to the floor.

Devnet, seeing my misfortune, announced with glee to the table, "Alice is a preteen."

To this the women erupted in drunken laughter while I stood there alone with my secret knowledge that a man had just exited this strange life forever. Sweet Thomas came to my rescue. He is a doctor now. ("Can you believe it?" Devnet recently said upon telling me that.) He jumped out of his chair and exclaimed that he would save the lobster. Across the floor he crawled, and picked the dead lobster up, spoke to it, said, "There, you little jumping clopper," and firmly placed it on my plate, then took my arm and walked me to my seat.

As we headed home, I rehearsed in my mind the way I would tell my father all that had happened. The man, the accident, and those words Devnet had said to me. But all I could get out was, "If a man told you to keep a secret or he'd kill your family, and he'd killed someone before, would you keep the secret?"

Maybe he was drunk, or tired. "Yes," he said without interest, and turned the country station up. Then, as we lowered ourselves toward mainland, my father saw something bobbing in the water.

"Holy shit, holy shit, holy shit," he said.

It was my father who went to the police, only after he'd gone into the water and dragged that poor lifeless body out. The headlights of my father's truck—just replaced that Saturday afternoon—were what lit that man up like an elevated ghost. The man was young; I could see that when he was upon the shore and my father had a flashlight on him. Dressed in a white shirt with a small, waterlogged notebook in his breast pocket. In the days to follow, everyone attributed my strange behavior to the fact that I'd seen a dead body. I had crossed a threshold, as Devnet had said I would.

---

Of course I thought of Devnet over the years. She, and not her father or young and dead George Collins, stood at the center of the awful night. So small and young, she seemed to have manipulated that entire episode and then just as quickly returned to her regular life. But I did not think of her in any tangible way. I did not say her name—not until the night this year when my husband and I went to the bad Mexican restaurant over on the pier. It's the only place open through winter. Summer you can get your picture taken in the booth and drive a bumper car, even take a train ride the three hundred miles around the lake. But darkness and cold set in and all you can get down there is a plate of greasy beans and cheese along with a margarita, which we like to do now and then just to get out of the house. My husband had three drinks that night. We sat at the bar and spoke to a man who believed he was a sailor just headed out on the big lake for his winter's catch. He looked the part, too, a gray beard and those remotely focused eyes, a bit of a limp. But of course the lake had been frozen for months. I didn't bother to say as much and nor did my gentle husband, which reminded me of why I had chosen him so many years ago. The man showed us his black tooth, said it was made of pure iron. Seeing that, my husband asked how it happened, and the man put his hand on my shoulder and gave a little wink and said, "We alls got secrets, doesn't we?"

My husband put his arm around me just then, pulled me toward him and laughed a bit. He was claiming me. No, he was saying. My sweet Alice don't have no secrets.

By the time we left the iron-toothed sailor, the snow had turned our small world to a plate of clouds. We cut easily through what had accumulated, which was at least an inch, and as my husband drove I watched our path in the rearview mirror. The tracks could have been those of a horse-drawn carriage, so silent they looked, and so quickly covered. When I looked ahead again we were about to pass the bridge to the point. This year there had been another accident on that bridge. The arch of it is so steep that it's like a jump, and if your car is moving fast enough it can catch a bit of air at the top. For generations teenagers have loved to press the gas to the floor and try to launch themselves in this way. This time the wheel got turned in the air, and those kids flew right over the side. They landed in the water and swam up one friend short. At the courthouse girls cried on the stands and their boyfriends shook but no one would say who'd been driving. I went to the hearings, every one of them, for I am a newspaper reporter. But I had not been over that bridge since childhood. Now I asked my husband to turn. He switched on that even-beating blinker and over we went.

The mansions were nearly all deserted, as they always are in winter. Our headlights created a strong but limited path, and in their tunnel I had a quiet feeling that a man would emerge like a ghost from the woods, causing us to slip on the ice and slide down the ledge and break through the frozen water. No such thing came to pass, and it was as we were headed back to the bridge that I glimpsed the letters on mailbox number 24.

"Stop," I told him. "Back up."

Why did he do that without question? The snow was falling so carefully, as though some invisible hand were guiding each flake down to the place of its eventual disappearance. That hand kept all snow from the name on the mailbox. Devnet R. Sawyer.

My husband drove us off the point. It wasn't until we were back on mainland that he asked me who lived there, if it was someone from the case.

Devnet Ricker her name had been. Surely this would be the same Devnet.

"Yes," I said to my husband, but only after the word was out did I realize that that might not be a lie, that not only had there been a Sawyer girl up on the stand, but there also had been that glamorously dressed woman with a long white cigarette waiting in the lot every single day. Her face had seemed vaguely familiar, but she had always fixed her gaze elsewhere, and quickly, when I appeared.

About a week after the drive with my husband, I returned to that mansion. I had expected to find Devnet standing at the great metal sink filled with lobsters, as though it were still that childhood day. Instead I found no answer at the front door, so I put it out of my mind, convincing myself that this was only a summer home, in spite of the fact that the walkway had been shoveled. It wasn't but three days later, when I went to a little shop to buy some Christmas presents, that there she stood, providing me with the sense of destiny fulfilled. She would not have spoken to me had I not spoken to her first. But we were in a small shop, I said her name, and she was cornered.

"Look at you!" she said. She flashed a large diamond my way and patted her curled bangs. A young daughter tugged at her arm and Devnet scornfully handed her a credit card. To the counter that daughter went, where she met her brother. The two of them had a heap of gifts. "I don't even know what they're buying!" Devnet said to me. "Probably all junk." She shook herself out and then leaned in and took my hand and said, "What are we, sisters? Second cousins or something? My daughter has your ears! Lacey, get over here, meet your aunt!"

As the kids bought their gifts, Devnet told me that she had just moved back to Kettleborough, that she went through a rough divorce but it was good to get out of Florida all the same, and look, she got to keep the ring!

"King's Point is where all my best memories are," she said. "Won't you come to our house? Please? For family's sake?"

The strangest part was that after the initial article of George Collins's mysterious death, the papers, too, deemed it a suicide. Apparently the police had received a phone call from a man who had known George Collins well. The man described George as depressed, said he spoke frequently of suicide, had had some trouble with his father, and had not left behind a note but had told the man before he went for the weekend at the lake that they would not ever see each other again. Back then it never did occur to me just who could have been behind that phone call.

Andrew Collins, the father, was reported to have said that his son had had a hard time of it lately, yes, very difficult.

A search for the driver? There was a note at the bottom of each article—contact the police if you have any information. There were only three articles. Our town is small. I never heard another word about it.

Yet I have followed Andrew Collins a bit. He worked his entire adult life as a history professor at the state university. Now he is retired, but he continues to keep an office on campus. After the accident of more than two decades ago he divorced and lost the other children to his wife, who moved out west, and he never married again. Just the way you would imagine an old professor, he walks down the hall with a hunch in his back and a finger to his mouth. He dresses in a V-neck sweater, and he always has a patch of hair in the hollow of his cheek, which he missed in his morning shave.


Though I had made a definitive plan to go to dinner at Devnet's house on Sunday, I appeared one day too early, in the late afternoon, because I couldn't bear the thought of an entire meal with her and her children. Devnet did not seem surprised. In fact, she was calmer than I knew she could be. She had a gift for me— a silver pendant with a moonstone at its center. She had made bergamot tea and as she poured she began to speak of the way her life in Florida had been filled with girlfriends. I tried asking her a few times if she had a teenage daughter but she plowed right over every word I said.

"Amanda Sawyer," I finally pushed. "This past fall on the bridge. That was your daughter?"

Devnet took her ring off then. She set it on the granite countertop. The large windows of the house face westward over the lake, and a beam of afternoon light fell upon that ring and sent it glittering throughout the room. Devnet pulled back her thick, curly hair and tied it in a knot at the base of her neck. Her skin had a look of too many hours in the sun. Silence, from her, was something profoundly sad.

"I saw you," she finally said. At the trials—I understood this much. She said she had also followed my articles. Since the trials, they had made a decision about the driver. An anonymous tip had come in, a man who claimed to have seen the driver. The boy denied the charge, but when he refused to offer another name in place of his own, he had been sent away. I had expressed misgivings about his guilt. I don't know why. I hadn't had the grounds for it and it had not been appreciated, not by the town or by the others at the paper.

Devnet began to make a low, faint sound, like the hum of a fishing boat.

One time I mustered the courage to speak to the father of George Collins. He was quiet and clear. He spoke precisely about the option of history as a major.

"My son," he'd answered, when I'd shamelessly asked who was in the photo on his wall. His son a hawk soaring toward that car, flying away nothing but a broken body.

"That man believes his son killed himself," I said now.

"Who?" Devnet asked. "I don't know who you mean." She retrieved her energy then, returned to the Devnet I knew. She said they'd thought of buying a condo up north, a place to ski and get away.

Yes, Devnet had been the first to claim suicide. But had she not thought of that, wouldn't her father have come up with it?

When she finished speaking of the condo she went to the refrigerator and filled a glass with crushed ice. That glass became her companion. She thrust it to her lips and bounced it, filled her mouth with ice and chomped, and then repeated the pattern again. In record time that glass was empty, at which point I said her name pleadingly.

She did not look at me. That faint sound returned, now so weak it could have been the dying squeal of an infant mouse. "Please," she finally said. It was a word that seemed to take all her strength.

Her daughter—of course it had been. I understood. I picked up the box with the pendant and then put it back on the counter. Though it's a small point, on the drive home I lost my way and felt certain, for a time, that I had been drugged. Round and round that point I drove with no sign of the bridge or the house where I had just been. When a black car with tinted windows passed slowly by me I began to shiver. How far did the power of Devnet's father reach? Finally I pulled over to the side of the road and breathed deeply, wiped the sweat from my brow. I was at a high spot and could see the open lake below. I got out of the car and stood in that biting wind and looked on at the vast, frozen water, waiting for a hawk to impossibly rise. I would end it now; I would track down Andrew Collins and tell him what I knew. For I could see it all: Thomas had said they'd seen the monster of the lake that day. My husband and I have not had children, and I am not sure we will. Because look, it is terrifying that the secret Devnet lived with had to get passed down to her daughter in this awful way. Terrifying, and just as unlikely as life sprouting up from only one infinitesimal seed, a drop of water, and our great sun.

# Secret

## 1972

AT SCHOOL ALICE met a boy named Gerald Hughes and this boy came to the fence behind her house. She put her hands on the rungs and he put his atop hers. It was a plain and bold gesture. There were rhododendrons that grew thick behind the fence, and Alice and Gerald crawled into them. They were fourteen years old and she ran her hands over his soft chest and they pushed their tongues into each other's mouths and they went to the woods and lay on a boulder that had been placed there one thousand years ago so that one day Alice could come to it and learn what it was to be a woman with a man.

"Have you ever—" she asked one day, and he interrupted her

to say that she had to come to his house for dinner before they could go all the way.

All the way, is that what she had meant to ask? Anyway, this was honor, Gerald Hughes meant for Alice to be his girlfriend.

His family lived in a railcar down by the river. Alice had known this before and that is why she did not sit with him at school lunch. To do so would be to cross a line that Alice understood should not be crossed in public. Gerald sat at the table of boys who stacked their trays high with food and drank carton after carton of milk and who may or may not have known that soon every last one of them would quit school.

Gerald Hughes's father had lost all his fingers, that's what they said. At school they said a lot of things about Gerald Hughes. The story was that Mr. Hughes had got drunk on his own creation and cut his fingers off at the sawmill and that Gerald's older brother had to quit school to hold the towel over his father's bleeding hands. Also that his father had found a canoe at the dump and driven his sons to Boston and put them, along with a case of beer, into the boat to paddle to their homeland. They ran out of beer not a mile from shore, the boat sprang a leak, and here in Kettleborough the family remained.

Alice had not expected him to have a mother, since there were no stories of her. But here she stood with a tray of gumdrop cookies. "I seen you in the papers," she said to Alice as she held the cookies forward. For skiing, she meant. Alice was on the local ski team and though she had never won first place, she had come in second or third a few times over the years, and this had occasionally put her on the front page of the paper. She took a cookie and smiled politely, and then, as she bit in, Mrs. Hughes looked her up and down and said, "Aren't you fancy." The cookie went dry in Alice's mouth and she did not know the full effect of the statement but she knew enough to want to flee.

His father had all his fingers, Alice saw that at dinner. The meal was warm and delicious, meatloaf and sweet cabbage and a pudding after, and at the table Gerald announced with pride and glee that his brothers had no chance at finding a wife but look at this, Gerald himself had already found a woman, a good woman for life. He sat up straight and his smile gleamed.

"Don't get ahead of yourself, son," his father said.

"This girl don't even know where she comes from," Mrs. Hughes said. She had not known, before Alice walked through her door, just who the girl would be. She had not asked. But she could see it now; even without the name her face said it clear as day. The Wickholms' little secret that everyone was meant to keep. Let those Wickholms sit up on their big hill in their big house with the view of their big lake and we down here will pretend we don't even know our own family. Not my family, Mrs. Hughes thought, not exactly, but might as well be. Valerie Hill had been her closest friend for life and if it weren't for what those Wickholms had done to Valerie, if it weren't for what they'd said, well. Val sat alone over in her big, empty house and here this grandbaby was and Mrs. Hughes had a mind to call her friend right up. Her husband saw it quick enough. He shot her a look and she stood and flattened her apron against her bosom and she began to stack the dishes as she said, "Don't you go having my son's babies. I don't care who you think you are and how good you think you are, my best friend, Val, had her baby at sixteen and that baby Jennifer disappeared but not before you showed up so I know what runs in your blood, don't you go having my son's babies."

Outside this small house the big dirty river lumbered down toward the lake. The evening light that bounced upon the water blinded Alice and there she sat, naked and revealed, that delicious hunger running through her blood. She and Gerald, all they had done together on the pine forest floor and all they had planned to do, none of it had contained an ounce of shame or love. Alice believed Gerald's mother had seen right through her. With this woman's eyes on her there was nowhere to tuck away that awful, shameful lust, or the real secrets, the ones Devnet had planted there. Those ones sat on her shoulder and whispered in her ear that she was wicked and that to her own father she did not belong. Keeping her eyes cast downward, Alice found her coat and with only one arm in it she fled from that small house.

Too good for my family, Gerald Hughes would think, for his mother's words would send Alice barreling so very far from his definite future. And isn't that what Mrs. Hughes had meant to have happen? She knew what it was to give her life over to this small place. Her boys would do the same but she would not wish it upon them. So there Alice went, out the door, good.

# Lake People

## 1974

THEY WERE ON a dirt road, the only sort her father liked to take. By way of dirt roads he frequently turned what may have been a fifteen-minute trip into one that took over an hour. As an adult Alice could describe these trips—in fact she did describe them—as her father's small attempt to awaken that man he had wanted to become. Freer, maybe that was it. Her mother had left when she was still a baby and he had always been alone in raising her and if he'd done a bad job of it at least he had done it, she could always say that. She reached up and turned the overhead light on and then shuffled through her pack and pulled out her math book.

"Do you know what the cops would think if they saw that light on? They'd think I put my daughter up to rolling a doobie." He laughed a small, self-conscious laugh, cleared his throat, and reached for the bottle that Alice knew he kept by the stick shift, under the papers and folders and empty clipboards. For a time when he'd had a girlfriend he had kept a bottle of wine there, along with plastic glasses. But never before had he grabbed the alcohol while Alice was in the truck, and he didn't now, either. Only touched it. Then he cracked his window and rolled it up once more. Heat blasted from the dashboard and the scent of her father tumbled about. Something quick—eucalyptus, or lemon—along with that sweet smell that she would soon learn to identify as bourbon.

This was their first trip to the Shaws' house—a grand old New England colonial that stood there like the dead end of a dirt road. But it wasn't the end—just before the house the road curved sharply eastward and continued down toward the lake. Yet situated as it was, and still is, it always looked as if the cars were headed straight for that house. And the house itself—if you were the driver, it looked as if that old house was coming toward you. It was not a feeling of terror the house cast but one of unrest. The house had stood for more than two hundred years, it had watched so very many carriages and cars lumber directly its way, and now that house felt as though it had taken in too much, and since it could not speak it could only emanate a distinct sense of mystery. Or at least that is how Alice felt in the days when she was sixteen and would go there with her father.

On that first trip, her father came upon the house too fast and had to jerk the wheel and turn the corner. That bottle slipped then and landed between his feet. He leaned forward and retrieved it, put it in his lap, and put the truck in reverse.

"Bad spot for a house," he said, and backed up.

They were parked backward in the driveway, and Alice looked out the back window, up the bed of the truck, and watched as the silhouette of a man emerged from the barn. In less than ten years that man would shoot himself in the head, and Alice would receive a note from her father to tell her as much, and even then, all those years later, it would still be this first image of him to come to her mind: Mike Shaw, skis set on his shoulder, walking definitively forward in the night. Her father opened the door of the truck and pushed his stiff body out.

"Don't just sit there," he said to Alice.

"Mike Shaw," he said to the man, and extended his own hand. Mike Shaw—at this point Alice hadn't figured that out. But she knew just who he was, everyone did. As a young man he'd gone west to ski, and then he'd gone on to the Olympics, where he'd won a silver medal. Practically the town hero, he was. The Kettleborough Museum had even hung a plaque in his honor, and Alice herself kept a picture of him in her dresser drawer, something torn from an old ski magazine.

He lowered the skis from his shoulder, handed them to the girl, and then said, "Hear you're quite the skier."

Alice nodded. A wet snow began to fall and sounds of a piano drifted about—June inside, playing a waltz on a winter's night. The men spoke for some time while Alice held those skis. Good equipment she had never known. The lining of her boots was torn and the buckles had been rigged together with wire. The bindings were always popping loose and though Alice was taller than most of the girls on the ski team, the other girls all had longer, faster skis. Her father took an envelope from his breast pocket and handed it to Mike Shaw.

"He gets them straight from the dealer," he said on the way home. "For cheap. It occurred to me one day."

He reached for his bottle then. They were at the crest of the hill, the east side of the Shaws' house still visible in the rear-view mirror. By the time her father mustered the courage—or whatever it was that took—to bring the bottle to his lap, they had coasted downward a distance and were near the lake. Alice's father steered with his knee while he pulled the cork out. He took a swig and then in a rush held it in her direction. Sweat covered her hand as she took hold of it. She tilted it to her lips but kept them closed, so none of the liquid entered her mouth. Only that sweet and brisk smell of her father, and a taste of the Carmex he rubbed on his full red lips. She handed the bottle back and the lake opened up before them, so vast and dark it looked like nothingness itself.

Alice's father had a habit of making a good, fast friend and keeping him for a few months, sometimes a year or two. Never a lifetime. Weekly he would go see these friends. Sometimes they would even spend holidays together. Mike Shaw became one of these friends, only this time, Alice was a part of the friendship.

They would arrive in the evenings, after her father picked her up late from school. Along those back roads and through the gray winter they would drive, silent. Though she knew the spot where the road curved sharply to reveal ahead that tall, looming house at the end of the tunnel of pine, each time the house appeared it seemed a shock.

Mike Shaw and Alice and her father would sit in their straight-backed, cushioned chairs in the parlor while a fire crackled behind them. Between them sat a copper table like none she had ever seen outside this room. Upon that table were olives and sharp cheese, sometimes shrimp and cocktail sauce, always a bucket of ice, and books, so many books. The liquor the men kept at their feet—Alice learned here that Mike Shaw preferred scotch, and her own father bourbon. Alice drank glass after glass of ginger ale, which June kept filled.

"June," Mike would call, when the ice or crackers or Alice's drink had run out. Sometimes Mike would look at Alice's father, wink, point his chin toward the kitchen, and say quietly, "Go on in there and fix her up, Paul. Make her laugh." Because June wasn't a part of this group. She stayed in the kitchen, loading the woodstove, sweeping across the room, stirring a pot of this or that—Alice never knew what, but would, for the rest of her life, recall that scent of garlic, sauerkraut, and sweet cream. In this way June would float, always in a thin dress that seemed out of place for winter. Her hair was thin and blond and she kept it tied in a loose bun at the base of her neck. To Alice, June seemed foreign. She wasn't—Alice had asked her father once, and he had roared with laughter. But she seemed that way, seemed as though this country was new and strange to her. It was the way she skittered in her own house, nervous about whether the place she set the bucket of ice down was right or not. She didn't bump into any doorways or the backs of any chairs, but always she seemed as though she just had. Even her communication didn't come out as full English, but as nervous strides toward a language. "More?" she would say, and point with trepidation at Alice's glass. "Ice you want?" It unnerved Alice, June removed like this, but that was their way, Mike Shaw's way. If she had been married to Mike Shaw, Alice thought then, she would have given him his way, too.


The men liked to talk about Steinbeck and Hemingway, and Alice's father would have gladly gone on without hearing her opinion, but not Mike Shaw.

"Tell me which books you've read," he would say.

Alice had read all these books, her father's favorite books. She stayed up late to read them.

"And which is best?"

She took a risk, offered one they hadn't said. "*The Catcher in the Rye*," she announced.

"Teenagers," her father scoffed.

Mike Shaw leaned back then, and drew in a long breath. He shook that angular glass and tipped it to his dark face to coax the last ice cube into his mouth. After that he took his time coming to his feet. He crossed the room and went to the built-in bookshelves on the far wall. From the highest shelf he grabbed Alice's favorite book, and flipped through the pages. She watched him inhale that impossibly clean but dust-like smell of a good old book.

"She's right," he said, and dropped the book in her father's lap. "The man can tell a story."

"That's right, too," Alice's father said, and gulped at his drink.

Besides skiing and books, the men liked to talk about sailing. "Men talk," June once whispered in Alice's ear as she filled her drink, but Alice ignored her. At the time, the men had been trying to recall the title of a particular book.

"*Kon-Tiki*," Alice said. She hadn't read that one, but she pretended.

"You're right," Mike Shaw said. "You're smart for your age. How old are you?" he asked, and walked across the room, to the fireplace. On the mantel was a framed picture of his two sons standing atop the ski hill on a gleaming blue day. He brought the picture to Alice. "Todd," Mike Shaw said, pointing to the taller one, and then, to the other, "and Scott. We send them away for school. June doesn't like it but I say it's good for them. Give them a little independence." He untucked his shirt, dusted the picture with its corner, and turned to Alice as he said, "They're good boys. Are they too old for you?" He turned back to the picture and stood there completely still, and then he looked abruptly at Alice's father, gave a little wink and laugh, and said quickly, "Am I too old for you?"

The first time Mike Shaw called their house, Alice was in the kitchen. She picked up the telephone and without announcing himself Mike simply asked her, "How are the skis?"

"Good," she said. She stretched the phone down the hall and into her bedroom, and shut the door. It was a wonder she did this so quickly. As though she had expected him to want to talk. As though she had prepared for it. "I don't have to push so hard for a turn," she said.

He asked her if she was winning any races.

"No."

"I don't know that it's worth it. Run, lift, takes all your time. Better you do something else. You have a boyfriend?" That last question, he asked it plainly, an afterthought. Alice told him she did not.

"Call me if you ever have any questions," he said. "About skiing."

"Okay."

"Or anything."

It was the first of many phone calls. Sometimes Alice would call him, and if June answered, Alice would hang up. But that didn't happen often, because she always took the telephone into her room at eight o'clock, and nearly every time, Mike Shaw called, just when she expected him to. They talked about skiing and they talked about books and Mike Shaw talked about the horrors of an ordinary life.

"Promise me you'll never drive a minivan," he said, and Alice believed she understood just what he meant.

"Your father is a good man," he said one time. "Not like me."

"You are good," she told him, and how fully she had meant that. To lift her up out of her lonely life, to make her feel she belonged, yes. "You are good," she repeated.

When Mike Shaw offered Alice a drink, she looked to her father for some advice, approval or not, though she knew nothing would come. Her father was at least ten years older than Mike Shaw, but in this man's house he became something small and unsure. Right now his eyes were cast upon the copper table. Alice imagined Mike Shaw taking her as his lover right there, across that table. Sometimes she imagined the two of them in the snow. She let his hand brush hers as she took the drink.

"Seven and seven," he whispered. "Don't let June catch that."

She drank it slowly, astonished by the hot path the liquid carved into her belly. It didn't make her feel dizzy or sick, as she had imagined it would, or like she wanted more, as the teachers at school had warned. It only entered her and remained, a small, secret confidence that she held. I am grown-up. I enjoy a drink. Never did she have more than one ice-filled glass.

But those drinks did certainly change her. No longer did she worry over what her peers thought. She looked into people's eyes and she said firmly what she meant.

"I'm going out tonight," she said to her father, and walked to the pier to meet Mike Shaw. Dry snow, the kind that would never accumulate, whipped along the frozen lake. Out across the way she could see a strip of darkness darker than the rest. Bear Island, she knew. Alice had never been there but frequently she imagined that island alive with all the ghosts of those lake people who had settled there nearly a century ago. Back when she was young, in the days when her father would tuck her into bed, he had told her the stories of those people, insisting that they still could be seen. Ida's widower, hovering beneath the ice with his window on a clear, still day; Eleonora at the tip of Bear Island with a lantern that shone like a pack of fireflies, just trying to stay warm. Over those stories that he would tell her Alice always felt some special claim, as though by the lake and its people she alone had been chosen. To be called so clearly into the water, to drop in and resume some watchful life with those people who lasted beneath—she could not help but imagine that. For that is what the lake people were to her—in all their stories, each of them had seen their fate before that fate came to pass. Nothing, not even death, had been illusive. Nor had anything been absolute. Alice wanted that.

"That's because you come from those people," Mike Shaw had said. She didn't know what he meant, but when he said that, Alice felt she had been seen.

Alone in the cold night she stood there waiting for him. A wind soared across the ice and curled up at her feet and sent her hair trailing like a river. As night moved on, that same wind began to howl like a solitary loon. He never did show up. Eventually she walked home and told her father that she and her boyfriend had watched a movie.

Sometimes they talked on the telephone about all the places in the world they would one day go. Sometimes they only held the phone to their ears, silent. "If you were my age," Mike Shaw said once, and also, "Once this wait is over." Alice wrote these sentences down in her journal, along with her very first love poems.

.     .     .

"I'll be damned," Mike Shaw said one evening. Alice's father's bottle of bourbon had long since run out, and now Mike held his own empty bottle of scotch at eye level. A wind rattled the old storm windows and found its way into her lap. "June," Mike Shaw called.

June came to the door and with the back of her hand wiped stray clumps of hair from her forehead. A dish towel hung from her fingertips.

"No more," she told him.

"Tomorrow, then," Alice's father said.

"No," Mike Shaw said. "We'll just run to the Spot." That was the little store on the lake, just down the hill from the Shaws' house. He slapped his thighs and came steadily to his feet and he walked through the doorway as though no one—especially not a woman he loved—stood there. This cast June tight against the wood frame. Past her like this, without a word, Alice and her father walked.

Though still no good snow had collected, Alice would remember that winter as one of bitter cold, that night so clear and crisp that she could have taken a knife and cut out squares of the air itself to store in her pocket. Mike Shaw opened the driver's door of his car, and her father opened the passenger's. Alice headed for the backseat, but shivered and remembered her coat.

"My jacket," she said when she entered the kitchen. June already had it in her arms. Rather than hand it to her, she held it up high, so that Alice had to turn around and ease herself into place. Once this was complete June placed her hands on the girl and turned her around.

"No hat," she said, and "Zip," she ordered. Alice did, and when she let go of the zipper June reached forward and cinched it up just a bit more. Then she stepped back and held a steady gaze on the girl. There was alcohol in her, and this felt somehow revealed as June stared. Yet June held no meanness in her look. No kindness, either, nothing but June staring into Alice and Alice staring into June for one long moment. Suddenly the woman shook her head and touched her palms to Alice's cold cheeks. When she released her hold, Alice returned outside.

"Take the front seat," Mike Shaw said. "Your father's gone into the barn." She didn't ask questions. Mike's skis, his pictures and medals, all of it—she knew it was stored in the barn. A light from the barn loft switched on, and as Mike Shaw put the car in reverse that light switched back off. Yet as the car backed out of the driveway, Alice gave no protest.

Later this moment would come to her as a tunnel whose sides suddenly fell open to reveal the great wide and growing universe. Snow had begun to fall, and lit up in the headlights those flakes looked like a galaxy that they drove farther and farther into. Yes, that was it. Alice had moved through that galaxy thinking the tunnel they carved marked the limits, but then the lights had gone out and a greater expanse had opened. There was sadness in that expanse, and regret, but there was also a real, true touch. For a moment there was. She would hold fast to that, and then move on to what her father must have done in the barn. How he must have picked up an old ski, angled it down, and pressed upon its middle. How he must have felt warm, for a time, and satisfied.

In the car, she didn't put her seat belt on. And Mike Shaw was drunk, of course, and she should have been scared to crash into a tree, to lose her leg or her entire life, but she wasn't. Which turned out to be fine.

As she would later imagine her father to be, Alice also felt warm that night. Her shoulders were relaxed, her hands comfortable in her lap. From the corner of her eye she watched Mike Shaw's shape, each deliberate shift he made, watched his loose but sure hands on the wheel. He cleared his throat and the sound replayed itself in her head. They weren't talking. Only riding quietly on a dark dirt road. Riding as a man and a woman did, should, she thought then. Though this man, she realized, didn't fill the car with any scent. Not even that of scotch.

"Reach into that glove box," he told her, and quickly pointed his chin toward it. It was a motion he frequently made. To Alice it said that under Mike Shaw's sharp instructions, life would be right. She did as she was told, feeling around a way to open the box, but before she figured it out he reached over and opened it himself. There was a gun in there, she saw that, though she said nothing. Also a pouch of tobacco, and this he removed. In it were a few cigarettes he had already rolled. "Light this for me," he said. She did, her first drag ever. The paper end ripped a little and a string of tobacco stuck to her wet lips. But she didn't cough. Alice knew enough not to cough. She handed him the cigarette. He smoked, and after a few puffs held it out between the seats for her to take again. She pretended that she had taken a cigarette a thousand times before. Mike Shaw breathed loudly and let his head tip back against the seat.

When the trees gave way it was to the lake. Here, at the end of the dirt road, was also the store. Though all the lights of the place were off, he pulled the car into the small lot, cut the engine, and left his headlights on. These lights created a tunnel of barren ice, and at the very far end of the tunnel she could see the dark edge of Bear Island. He must have known, she would realize later. June, too. They must have known the store would be closed.

Mike Shaw reached down and pulled a lever, and in a rush his seat rolled back. With a loud breath he stretched his legs out, patted his thighs. He smoked his cigarette lightly, not like he needed it but like it offered him some small pleasure.

"You know how hard it is yet?" he asked.

"Yes."

"You're smart for your age," he told her. "For any age I suppose." The cold air that came into the car felt good, fresh. As did sitting there, talking with Mike Shaw, who had chosen her. When a truck drove by she tensed, but Mike did not. He only switched the lights off and unrolled his window all the way. It was teenagers in the truck, and they slowed down to throw beer cans out the window and hoot. To this Mike Shaw opened his car door, dropped his cigarette, and stepped on it. Then from the ground he picked up one of the crushed beer cans the boys had thrown and like a rock skipped it toward the lake. When he closed the door of the car again, he reached into his pocket and withdrew a flask, handed it to Alice. It was nearly full.

"When you get married," he said. "Or maybe you shouldn't. Maybe you'll use that brain of yours and understand what's right for a man and what isn't."

"I won't marry," she said. (She would, of course, more than once, the first in not too long a time. And it would be to a good-enough man, though not a man entirely unlike Mike Shaw. A man who, like Mike Shaw, had more than a decent amount of himself. A man who won races and women, a man who would wander. And she would wonder whether she should have chosen another, chosen a man with softer, much softer hands.)

"Don't," Mike Shaw said. Her teeth clenched and in the darkness her legs began to shake with cold. Soon her whole body shook. "It's all work and doing this and doing that," he said. "None of it is important. When I used to ski," he said.

"You still can ski."

"That's what I like about you." He put his hand on her head. A father may have put his hand there like that. Not her father, but a father. "I used to feel so a part of it all," he said.

Alice didn't respond. Which, for Mike Shaw, turned out to be the right thing. In the silence his hand moved down from her head to her shoulder, then across her arm, onto her thigh. She took one long gulp from the flask. By the time his rough-bearded face breathed warm air against her cheek, the alcohol had opened and spread in her stomach. Though she could no longer see the island before her, she kept her vision fixed in that direction. The flicker of a light at its tip, for a moment she thought she saw that, though it may have been a trick of the eye. What happened happened quickly. In too quick a time to eat dinner, do math homework. But had it been a ski race, and had Alice followed behind another skier, crossing the finish line after him, with the time between the skiers the same as the time it took what happened to happen, the winner would have taken first place by a considerable amount. This she knew. Of course she had been a virgin. Mike Shaw started the car and they returned to that tall house in the road.

That night, her father did not say goodnight to Mike Shaw. He simply opened the truck door for his daughter and closed it once she'd climbed in. "Buckle up," he told her, his voice weak and his breath a fog across the cold truck. As he drove he reached his hand in her direction, let it hover above her leg for one moment. Heat blew hard against their faces and sent the quick and sweet smell of him circling around. They never went to see Mike Shaw again.

But they did take the long way home. Her father drove slowly, and as they passed alongside the lake he unrolled the window. Alice imagined floating out that window, landing upon the frozen water and being taken in as one of the lake people. At the pier he stopped and turned the truck off. Her coat was cinched tight and her arms hung awkwardly over her lap. She looked like a child just in from the snow.

"There," her father said quietly, and pointed out to the island. The lake was illuminated, a radiant white, everything crisp and immovable. "Eleonora's lantern. Do you see it?"

The wind picked up and howled like a loon. Alice looked out toward the tip of the island. Of course she saw nothing, but still she nodded in agreement. Yes, she was saying. Yes, I know that light is there.

# PART THREE

# Hill Country

## 1981–1982

THE FIRST TIME she went to his place there was no staircase—
and how would her life have turned out had that staircase never
been built? Because funny is what he had been. So funny that
she would be knocked right over.

He lived one hundred miles north of the lake, beyond the
mountains, in a vast spread of land where even the tourists didn't
go. After she'd met him, it took Alice but one week to show back
up in his driveway. There, on his land, at dusk, in the distance
the mountains hung like a single stair across the skyline.

"I wanted to see the mountains," she said, which in a way was
true, but the real truth was of course that she had wanted to see

him. He opened his arms and took her in and the motion was certainly one filled with mocking but still there she was in his arms. They stayed up through the night, telling each other stories and lying back on his bed, keeping the time from passing by keeping their eyes open to each other. When the sun burrowed into the room they looked at nearly all they could look at of each other. Later, he took her to the thrift store, bought her some silly, cheap clothing, said, "Look at that, now you don't even have to go back home."

Later still he said to her, "See, I got room."

"Some man thinks you're a good lay so you just move in with him?" her father asked her when she phoned.

"Yes," Alice said. She did not go home.

He had a great plume of blond hair and he was tall and so funny. From his bedroom—from his bed, even—she could see the mountains. After they made love he would stand there in the second-story window and pee right out of it. And then one time he pointed to a ledge miles away, up the mountain, and he said, "There, let's do it there." The birch trees were aglow and they drove and hiked and made love in that spot he had pointed to, on the hard rock ledge, and certainly she and Josh understood each other in some ancient way.

That first time she'd met Josh, Alice had watched him, eavesdropping. He'd been talking to a friend. That they were talking of some old girlfriend of Josh's was clear. Their subject was not. "Bad news woman," Josh had said, and then, "She's had like five of them." Miscarriages, Alice had thought suddenly. The word had dropped into her mind like an early leaf turned and fallen. Just as quickly it blew away. When, years later, she recalled that moment, she would have to remind herself that she hadn't really heard the conversation anyway.

. . .

"You don't love me," Alice said one morning at breakfast.

"Ah, baby, no."

"I love you," she said. She had said it to him before. And in her lifetime she would love again, in a deep, deep way, but never again would it be like this. Here her heart had been wide open. Do what you will, she might have said.

Josh filled his fork with eggs and hash browns and like an airplane he pushed it toward her mouth. Zoom, zoom, open up. She did, and laughed. He paid the check and waited for her in the truck.

They made love in that truck. On the mountain, in the truck, upside down, in the kitchen, in the bathtub.

On that drive home she thought he was angry. She believed this would be it, she had ruined it. It had happened before. "I don't want a girlfriend," he would say. "Stay here, be my pal. You're my bud. Stay, live with me." That and, "I want to die a lonely old man. I don't want a girlfriend." Okay, she would say, every time. How could she say that? It only took a few days, anyway, before he wanted her in his bed again. Each time she agreed. So now, on that drive home, she thought it would be that way. She stayed quiet. She squinted into the thick woods, let her vision shift just enough for a stone wall to appear, a lake, a rising hill of maple like those of Kettleborough. In these moments when he left her she had learned to do that.

But on this day she was wrong. They stopped at the only stoplight in town and something hit her and she turned to find him pelting her with little packets of cream. Back at the restaurant, just for this, he had filled his coat pockets. One of his jokes. For a time in the renovations of the house—it was a daily chore, and still undone—the bathtub had been in the middle of the room. It had a showerhead, and a curtain that enclosed the entire tub, and Alice had been in there when suddenly a banana flew over the top. Another. And then a potato, a loaf of bread. She had laughed and laughed and the food had not stopped and she had even laughed when the frozen chicken hit her in the head.

Now he pulled into the courthouse and turned the truck off and came around and opened her door and lifted her out, carried her to the steps. It was deep fall, the leaves a fire raging through the valley.

"Whoops," he said, and dropped her on purpose. Ha, ha. He made a show of picking her back up, and at the top of the steps he dipped her and kissed her and said, "Aw, how romantic," and they were married.


Among the things that Paul sent his daughter when he heard the news were rubber boots, a rain jacket, and a good rain hat that tied beneath the chin. "Now that you're a farmer," he had written. Was it mocking? Alice liked to believe it was not, though she knew that her father was upset and would not ever come visit. In the years since Alice had gone to college, Paul had become angry and stubborn. But it was true—Alice and Josh had planned to farm—chickens, they spoke of, and gardens, and even perhaps a goat. But what did they know? Winter had come but no snow, only so much rain that the ditch along the side of the road had transformed to a dirty river. In it were carried brittle leaves and sticks and once in a while a beer can, an empty bag of chips that a driver had let float out the window.

Josh worked most days, construction here and there, but Alice couldn't find a job. She took to passing her time sitting close to the woodstove—for there were still great gaps between the logs that formed the walls of the house, which meant that the wind came streaking through like an army of ghosts. Alice read and cut the crosswords from the paper. They had built a staircase by now, together, during one of their good spells, and she learned to keep a packed suitcase at the base of it, for even now that they were married Josh's periods of breaking up with her still had not ended. She believed the suitcase helped to put Josh at ease about their marriage.

Her father might not approve, but those gifts he had sent were sensible. Each day Alice put them on, the boots and coat and hat, and went out into the cold, wet world. It was her one grace of the day. Up the road she walked. She dreamed of leaving, of going to Boston and getting a job, taking up an apartment in the city. Though in truth what propelled this dream was the vision of Josh chasing her there. Alice, he would call. How he would tell her he loved her.

Alice liked to call to animals, like the moose she saw one day as she stood in the window. She spoke to it silently: *Come here, I won't hurt you, come inside.* The beast loped across the lawn and was off. None of the animals—there were a lot, like deer, and the coyotes she heard howling in the night—would respond to her. None but the squirrel who now came to the back door each morning and waited for her to put breakfast out. She fed it toast spread thickly with jam. But she had yet to befriend any other animal. Even Josh's dog, Dorie. When Alice tried to bring her along for a walk she would show her teeth and faintly growl. For friendship Alice stuck to the squirrel.

And then one day she was walking through the field across the road and speaking in her head to a deer she was sure she heard over at the edge of the thin line of woods, by the road. Josh wanted to call it off. He had moved to his own bedroom. Alice could call it off. She could, couldn't she? She cinched her rain cap tighter and took big, heartfelt steps, though her hip was still sore.

"Martha!" a woman called. *Maatha.* Not a deer at all. "Martha up the street! That's me!" The woman moved quickly through a patch of brambles and ran across the field to Alice. Under her sweatshirt her massive chest heaved.

"It's Martha up the street," the woman—sopping wet, with no hat or coat or boots—managed between breaths. "Alice! I been meaning to see you, I says to my husband, I says Ronny, that over in the Blaisdells' old place, that is Miss Alice Thorton, nicest girl I ever knew. I says that! Course I see you gots yourself a man, so you isn't Thorton no more, but all the same I says it was you and sure enough plain as day it is, I ain't so stupid as Ronny says, but of course I don't get out much, first day really, the kids, you know Christy? Fourth grade already! And Jason first and today I say, what the hell. Ronny's sleeping the day over at the factory, your husband work there, too? Course! Why else we come to this forsaken place! My Ronny works nights and sometimes he sleeps there, just a little cot they got, but here I am gabbing on and you ain't said one word. Gabbing Martha, that's what my sister says. Shut your trap! Ronny says that. Just shut up. Alice."

Alice Thorton, it was still her name. She had not had the courage to take Josh's, had thought it would be too much for him and would make him leave her. Now she wondered if the name would give her a bit of authority. The wind shifted and a deer took flight out of the woods. Alice watched as it cut across the field and was gone. That was it. "Martha."

"Martha Paquette," Martha said.

Martha Hill, she had been. In Kettleborough nearly all the Hills—no one knew just how many—lived up there by the dump. Hill Country, they called it. Not the Hills themselves but others about town, because the road seemed as though it was its own country. Across their spread of land were strewn houses and shacks and even teepees. A thin stand of pine trees lined the road before their property, so to see in one had to try. And people did, momentarily, slowing down and edging toward the side of the road, peering but pretending not to. There were rumors about how the Hills guarded their land with shotguns, so no one ever dared pull in. So Alice hadn't really known Martha, not until they had been placed together for a school shop project. In spite of herself Alice had loved Martha's unflinching ways. "Kids don't like me, ain't that life?" she would say. That year there had also been rumors about Martha, of her home and the kind of meat she ate, raccoons mostly, and then those terrible things, her doing it with Jay Hubbard one minute and his brother the next, on the old railroad bed with a makeshift condom of plastic wrap and a rubber band. Alice had done nothing to stop those rumors, though in shop class she and Martha had laughed together so much that whispers started to circulate about her, too, ones that said that Alice was finally with her own kind. Still, when Martha would wave in the hallway or the cafeteria, Alice would turn the other way. This was public, after all, where Hills were only friends with Hills. It wasn't long before shop class ended and so, too, their friendship.

"I always thought of you," Martha said now. "I says to Ronny, I says, I know I got me a friend in Alice Thorton. And up here we need a friend, don't you say? My family ain't up here, course you know that. I know you always was nice. I says, Ronny Paquette, just because you can't stand me don't mean no one can. You leave this house, he says, and I'll whoop your ass. And he will, too, ain't that the truth." Here she turned her bare face into the wind and made a whistling noise, yes-sir-ee. "But today I says what the hell, Martha Paquette, we is taking ourselves for a walk. And here I run into you! Our house first one up from the gully, you know that? You seen it? You's the nicest friend I ever had, you know that, Alice Thorton?"

"I've seen your house, Martha," Alice said. Each day she

passed by it, a small turquoise house down in the gully, with rooms built on from the center so sloppily it looked like a house of playing cards that would surely blow over in the wind.

"Sure," Martha said, responding to nothing. "I would love to take a walk with you tomorrow." At the edge of the field Martha called Alice's name once more, and it came to Alice not like the insistent voice of this strange old friend but like a welcome song, or a bell. A warm wind came up behind Alice and her hair blew forward, caught in her mouth. She turned southward, knowing that if she crossed those mountains she could just go a distance and then fall right into the lake, home.

While Josh split firewood in the dark, Alice fished through the kindling box for another old newspaper to cut the crossword from. Already they had a pile of firewood big enough to last two winters, but still he wouldn't quit. Over the kindling box Alice sharpened her pencil with a knife. When the phone rang she was startled, and the knife slipped, and she nearly sliced her finger open. In a daze Alice counted the phone's rings and imagined what may have happened had that knife slipped differently, or just a little more. She may have sliced her wrist right open. She may have bled to death. Then what would Josh have thought? They had no answering machine, and at thirty the phone still rang.

"Yes," she said. Not the way she typically answered the phone but this is what came out.

"Martha up the street," the voice on the other end whispered. "Martha. You there? Alice? It's Martha up the street!"

"Yes."

"Thank the Lord for that. I gots to tell you something, Alice. You know my husband, you know Ronny. I gots to pack his dinner and sometimes his lunch, too. You ever been to the mill? Over past town? Alice? They got those machines there to buy some boxes of soup but I say Ronny! Alice? Hello?"

"Martha."

"I thought you dropped right off the planet!" The whisper vanished. Martha talked full-speed now, told Alice that tomorrow she needed to make cookies for her husband's lunch—and of course she'd slip two each into her children's packs, too—but she was out of flour. Did Alice have a few cups of flour? A little more than that? Enough for the week? "You know Ronny. He says I leave this house my ass is grass. Dead meat. Dead as a doornail? You remember that from school? Dead As A Doornail!"

"Yes, Martha. I'll bring it up in the morning."

Alice set the phone down, fed the fire, drank a glass of water. The room was big and empty around her, and when the phone rang—Martha again—she was thankful. "My clothes all wet from our walk today, you remember?" Martha said she could not have her husband catch her with wet clothes. Could Alice come over and take them, just hang them to dry for the night at her own house?

"Martha," Alice said. "Isn't your husband home now?"

"You think I'm on the phone when Ronny's home? He works nights, I got to tell you twice!"

"Then can't you dry the clothes at your own home?"

"What if he comes in for a surprise! Alice, use your brain!"

Alice agreed to do it. In truth she was relieved to have a task. She put that big-brimmed hat on and Josh's thick jeans, the ones lined with flannel. She pulled her feet into her boots. There was something the matter with her car, it had not started for weeks, so she took Josh's truck keys from his coat pocket. She would go to Martha's first, get the wet clothes. And then to the grocery store, where she would buy the woman her flour. Before leaving,

Alice went to look in the mirror. How many days had it been since she'd been in public? Her face looked different, tired, the skin pale and blotchy. She pinched her cheeks until they filled with blood and then she went out, passed by Josh without a word. He did not look up from his work.

There was a small wooden porch that led to Martha's front door, and Alice went up it and knocked, but there was no answer. She could hear the television, and see its flashes of light through the curtains. She knocked again, and called out, "Martha!" and that was when she heard a pounding on the window, followed by the holler of a little boy. Alice moved toward the window where he had knocked, but the curtain had been pulled shut again.

"Get," she heard. It was a low sound, a sort of hiss. It had come from Martha, her head stuck out the front door, darting back and forth like a bird on watch. With her foot she pushed the door open farther, and opened her arms. The pile of wet clothes dropped. "Get," Martha said once more, and pulled the door closed.

Alice considered leaving the clothes there on the porch, but then what else did she have to do? She took the clothes and though Martha had been cruel she went to the store for her all the same, bought a big bag of flour. At home she realized that she could have gone to the store first, then dropped off the flour when she picked up the clothes. The way she had chosen to do things was probably more difficult. But at least this way filled up more of her time. Carefully Alice hung the sweatshirt, T-shirt, and jeans on the dry rack. They were still soaked and wrinkled, and they already smelled of mildew. It seemed Martha had taken them off and stuffed them away as they were. Alice took them back off the rack and put them in the machine to wash. She unlaced the sneakers and pulled the tongues up and she set them by the woodstove.

Josh's father called him that night. What they talked of Alice never knew exactly, though some of it had to do with money. His family lived all the way in Idaho, where he had grown up, and Alice knew nearly nothing of them. Only that his mother prayed, that his father was a businessman, that he had two sisters. When he hung up the telephone and came to the kitchen he took the crossword out from under Alice's pencil, put her coat on her lap, and told her they were going for a walk. She wore that hat, too—for some reason she would always remember that detail. That hat fastened under her chin, keeping the rain out while they walked down toward the gully. There was an old freezer down there, on the side of the road. It had come from Martha and her husband—Alice would learn that soon. It had broken down and Martha and Ronny meant to take it to the dump, so they hefted it up into that flatbed truck and Martha told her husband no, that will fall right out the back, we need to fasten it. Shut your trap, he had told her. Shut your damn pie hole. And it fell out! Martha would say repeatedly, when she told the story to Alice. Fell out right there at the base of the gully, right as they started up the hill.

On the walk Josh talked of his father, how he was aging. Alice knew then that the spell was over, he would come back to her today. Her hip hurt dreadfully and at first she had made an effort to make sure he knew that, but now she did the opposite. When the rain collected in the rim of her hat she reached up and let it pour out slowly, right down the middle of her face. With her eyes crossed she watched these drops in the dim moonlight. Josh leaned in, his hands tucked inside the opening of her large coat, and rolled himself a cigarette. They shared this though Alice never smoked. The lights were on in Martha's house, and when Alice stopped to look on at it Josh stopped with her. He didn't know about the walk, the phone call, didn't yet know anything about Martha. For now Alice kept this, something for herself. Flickers from the television found their home in the curtains.

Josh said, "Some asshole lives there." Alice said nothing, they walked on, and in time he said, "We're having sex tonight."

And they did, with the lights on. "I want to remember you," he told Alice.

In the morning Alice got up quickly and bathed, got dressed as though she had somewhere important to go, though in truth it was only up the hill to Martha's. Still, it was something. She had considered keeping the flour to herself, waiting for Martha to apologize, but what good would that do? She put the bag of flour in a big wicker basket, along with Martha's clean and dry clothing, and she laid a plastic grocery sack over the top to keep it all dry and she walked up the hill humming.

It was raining still, of course it was. Out of habit Alice cursed the rain, but in truth didn't it make those woods green? Such brightness in winter—for that alone the rain was worth it. And the water, the way it rushed down the hill and even her own body. Perhaps, Alice thought as she walked down toward the base of the gully and past that rusted freezer, she and Martha could take a walk in all this rain. Perhaps they could walk over the mountains and down, all the way to the big lake.

"Shh," Martha hissed when she opened the door. Alice had the basket hung from her arm. Martha's head shot out the window and looked in both directions, again a terrified animal. "Leave it," she snapped. She pointed and then pulled the door closed. With something akin to shock Alice moved to set the clothes and flour where Martha wanted them. When she bent forward there was a slight tap at the window. She turned and saw Martha rush that curtain tight once more.

Alice walked slowly toward home. It was going downhill that made her hip hurt the worst. Josh was at work and before Alice lay one more empty day. With those logs missing from the walls the house was too cold to move about in. She could sit by the woodstove or she could get in the bathtub. Or maybe she would just get back into bed. Curl up. Die.

No. No, no, no.

Alice hadn't even taken her boots off when the telephone began to ring. Martha. In time, when Alice is remarried and happy, her husband sleeping next to her and a fire at the far end of the bedroom, the phone will ring before dawn and Alice will think, Not Martha again. Though of course by then Martha will be long gone. But she will think that, which will also mean that when, in her half sleep, she curls toward the warm body beside her, she will for a moment take it for Josh, and not her good, true husband.

"Martha up the street!" Martha says it as though it is their first communication of the day.

"Yes," Alice said.

"Just checking in. You know what my daughter says to me? She's in the fourth grade and she is a smart whippersnapper, that's what Grammy Hill calls her. Christy, anyway, she says, Missy Mom, that's what they call me, Christy and Jason both, they say, Missy Mom? This time Christy says, Missy Mom, you know I am old enough to sit here next to Jason and keep him watching the boob tube. She says she thinks I can go out for a walk at night with my best friend and I say what the heck, Christy, you are one good cookie."

"Okay," Alice said.

"Okay? Truly you promise?"

"Yes, Martha."

"Wait! I know you got a forgetting mind. I told you how many times? No one allowed on our porch! That is the Rule of Ronny, me and the kids say that. No one allowed on the porch and now twice you walked on it. You just wait this time. Eight o'clock? Ronny says he's coming home from ten this morning until seven at night. Don't come between then! You just wait on the street when you come, I'll watch for you, Alice. Alice?"

"Yes."

"Okay," Martha said. "Thank you for the invitation."

Alice hung up the telephone and turned the oven on. It was cold but she would bundle up and she would move about the house, sweep and maybe put up a decoration or two, and then she would make some cookies for Martha and her children.

Which she did, over and over again. Nearly a month passed in this way. Alice now had a friend, and besides, she and Josh were in a good phase. He had brought a plastic ring home for her and with pride she wore it on her finger. Nights they lay facing each other, legs twined together, and they spoke as though it were their first meeting. They told stories about childhood and stories about their futures, the gardens they would plant and the countries they would visit. Josh told stories about his day, the fool he had made of himself when he made a joke that no one laughed about. You would have laughed, he said to Alice. Which was true, it was what they had. When times were good they could not stop, over and over again Alice and Josh made each other laugh.

Martha was their only trouble. Not because Alice had taken to going for a walk with her every night—that wasn't a problem because she did not tell Josh about it, she simply went for a walk and pretended it was on her own. But the telephone, the way it would not stop ringing. Martha up the street, I need some flour. Martha, I'm out of sugar. Do you think you can bring over a cup of milk? Just Martha, wanted to see that you slept all right. She called before they were out of bed or after they had gone to bed, and often she called twice with less than five minutes in between. If they did not answer Martha would just let it ring. She was patient in that way.

"Alice doesn't want to talk to you," Josh said once. Also, "Don't you call here again."

"Your husband ain't so good to you, is he?" Martha said on one of their walks. Martha who was not allowed to leave the house. Martha with a bruise like an under-ripe plum across her neck. Still, Alice had not been able to answer the question.


"I got a letter today," Alice said now to Martha as they walked. It was just past Christmas. How Martha had looked forward to that holiday. She had made an Advent calendar for Alice and Josh out of construction paper and pictures that she cut from magazines. Josh had made fun of it but each morning like a prayer Alice had opened one more window. Martha had hung thin cardboard snowmen and Santa Clauses in the windows of her own house, and one afternoon when Alice walked by she watched as Ronny strung up colored lights while Martha stood on the porch clapping. It was Alice's first view of Ronny, though it wasn't a good one, for he had been on the ladder. Still, he looked smaller than she'd imagined, and somehow kinder. He turned as Alice walked past and he tilted his head downward, a sort of wave. Not Martha, though. She kept her focus on her husband.

"Ain't that something?" Martha said now. She said that she loved mail more than most anything in the world. Her mother had sent her a Christmas package, she said, and in it there were cookies. "Just the taste of home, and still fresh. Some days I just wait and wait for mail." Martha's voice moved far away, turned steady and serene. It was not a voice Alice had known Martha held within.

"I do, too," Alice said firmly. In fact, it was just what she'd been doing when today's letter arrived: sitting there in the chair by the woodstove and looking out the window, waiting for the mail lady to come by. Usually it would be junk mail for Josh, maybe a bill. Perhaps if she had taken his name she would have felt entitled to open his mail, but as it was she would just set it on the table for him. Mail for Alice had come only once, but still she held hope for something more. And today it came. Nowadays her hip was only a dull pain, she could run, and she did just that, back to the house with the envelope tucked into her shirt. No return address, though she recognized her father's writing. She had not been prepared for what was inside.

"It was an obituary," Alice told Martha. "A man I used to know from Kettleborough. Did you ever know Mike Shaw?"

"Todd Shaw, don't you know him?"

"No."

"I don't know, maybe they're related, who knows. Don't you know Todd from school?"

"No."

"He ain't in our grade anyway, he's one ahead, and anyway he went to private school for high school. Todd Shaw, I had a true-life crush on him! Nicest boy in our school, I told him that the day he left. I says Todd Shaw, you is nice to everyone, even me. Then I hit him on the shoulder, I always remember that. I says Todd, you don't have to go all red in the face! Mike Shaw his brother or something, I don't know."

"No," Alice said. "I don't know."

"Who sent it to you?"

"What?"

"The obituary, Alice! Who sent it?"

"My father."

"What father?"

"What?"

"Nothing. Swore on my life."

"Okay."

"Alice! Aren't you going to ask me again?"

Alice shrugged.

"Okay then. My lips are sealed." Martha swiped her fingers across her mouth and made a motion to throw an imaginary key away. Then she said, "You know the Wickholms in Kettleborough?"

"What? Up on the hill."

"My aunt and uncle and cousins live right below them. You know what else? I know a secret about the Wickholm family."

"What is it?"

"I ain't telling, swore on my life."

"Okay."

"Aren't you going to ask me again?"

"Martha," Alice snapped. They had reached the top of the hill above Martha's house. Weeks ago Martha would have been breathing hard, and Alice, too—though not as hard as Martha—but now they could both walk right up the hill without missing a breath. "He shot himself," Alice said.

"Mr. Wickholm!"

"Martha, no. Mike Shaw. The obituary. He shot himself." The ground was wet and bright green against the patches of brown mud, and upon everything there sat a layer of gleaming water. And the smell of it all—from the depths the water pulled up that full earth smell.

"Well," Martha said. She clapped her hands together and

looked upward, then pointed. A woodpecker large as a hawk was there in the tree above them. For a moment they watched that bird working. Around the base of the tree woodchips had formed a wide ring. Martha took Alice's mittened hand. As far as Alice could remember, it was the first time they had touched. It wasn't sympathy that Martha held her hand with, or anything like sentimentality. Instead it felt to Alice like pure instinct, and awe for that bird. After a time Martha said, "Well, ain't that a mistake." Mike Shaw's suicide, she meant.

"Yes," Alice said. And somehow, with Martha there at her side, Alice felt it really could be as simple as that.


In late January Martha called with a plan. Her son, Jason, had heard about it at school—on a full moon the ghost of the train conductor walks the abandoned tracks down in the gully in the woods.

"He'll carry a lantern," Martha said. "Jason knows three people seen it themselves. And once the ghost of the train itself!" For a moment Martha was silent. They were on the telephone, and her silence was so unusual that Alice, too, said nothing. After some time Martha said, "That ghost train whooshing by and disappearing. If it weren't for my children, I'd jump right on that train. Ride it straight into disappearance."


There were two more weeks until the full moon, and in that time the rain let up and then one night snow came down lofty as a cloud. Alice walked out into the gleaming night and there across the way Josh emerged from the snowfall, his appearance so unexpected that he may have been walking out of another world entirely. He crossed the snow to Alice and together they stood within those impossibly and perfectly shaped snowflakes and they were in love then, easy and pure.

On the day of the full moon Alice kept the radio on while she made cookies for the midnight outing she had planned with Martha. All day the announcer spoke of the ice storm that would come. She should have paid more attention to it. Josh, too. He knew the storm was coming but that was not what he worried over—it was the woman. Bad news, he'd taken to calling her, just as he had called some unknown woman that first day Alice had watched him. That day now seemed years ago, and Alice years beyond it.

You don't have to be Martha's friend, Josh would say. Do you even like her? Is she smart, Alice? Alice, you do not have to go out in the middle of the night for some stupid escapade she's planned. Also, what if that husband of hers comes home? He could shoot you, couldn't he?

Alice should have listened to that, too.

She would have liked some real reason to not go. Not because she wasn't interested—a small place in her really did believe such a vision possible. Yet it would have meant something to have a reason to not go. My husband would like to spend time with me. My husband wants to make dinner together, love. He cannot sleep if I am not there next to him. A reason like that, Alice had no such thing. She waited for the cookies to cool before wrapping them in wax paper and tucking them into the backpack. She put in a blanket and a thermos of tea. Josh spent the evening reading in the bedroom, and when Alice went in to say goodbye he pretended—she could tell—to be asleep.

Martha was already waiting in the street, and she had her two children behind her. She held a flashlight pressed up against her chin, and the light made her skin a glowing, translucent red. In it her blue veins were revealed. The effect was sickening and her children laughed.

All these weeks, and Alice had never met Martha's kids. She had not known she would meet them tonight, and their presence sent a quick fear through her. But Martha was their mother, wasn't she? She was an adult.

"I heard so much about you," Christy said on the way up the hill. She took Alice's hand just as a wet snow began slowly to fall.

At the top of the hill above Martha's house they turned off into the woods, and for their family, walking through the trees could have been walking through a foreign country. They clung together and were silenced, their mouths agape. The woods were lit up with moonlight and there was no need for the light Martha had brought.

Alice had been here before, to the place where the easy stretch of land drops abruptly downward, to the old tracks. Just before that spot the woods come to a halt and a great strip of granite begins. Up this they climbed, to its wide summit. Here Alice opened her pack and withdrew the blanket, tea, and cookies, and Martha said, "You done outdid yourself!" Then Martha gathered her children in her lap and sat down and stared forward. When the wet snow turned to a steady, insistent rain, Alice asked if they might like to go back, but it was as though Martha had lost all hearing, all peripheral vision, too, everything except what was focused directly forward, into the base of this deep-woods gully. Martha didn't have a hat on but she did not seem to mind the rain, not even when it turned to ice and began to pelt their faces so hard it could have been aimed right at them. Her children didn't complain. Intently with their mother they waited for the ghost.

And they believed it came, all four of them believed that.

Alice for years believed in it. It wasn't until she was in her fifties, on a day when thoughts of Martha filled her to the brim, that she realized what their vision that night might have been. That was when she went to the museum in Kettleborough that was housed where the train station used to be. They'd had a special exhibit that day, of the animals that used to roam this eastern land. So it was a lost herd of elk, she would decide.

But Martha and her children would never have a chance to decide that. And couldn't it be better that way, to believe so simply in what they had seen? Alice had been fussing with her rain cap when she heard that involuntary noise of wonder fall from Martha. She looked forward, and there at the base of the gully a wild beast came forth as though from behind a curtain of black draped from the sky. Like an apparition that animal shone. She had a beard of white and she walked with grace upon the iced ground. One by one a pack of children came out of the rain to follow their regal mother. How she glowed, she could have been carrying a lantern. Alice and Martha and the children were together transported.

None of them ever spoke of it. Those beasts finished their walk along the track and Alice and Martha and the children rose.

On their walk home the ice stopped shooting in pellets and instead fell straight down upon them, as though whatever valve there had been in the sky had broken. Already the road was glazed over. Power would soon be out. Over at the mill, no, they could not be working. Ronny would be on his way home, or already there. Of course Martha realized this, too—probably even the children did. Together they locked arms and slid their way downward.

But Martha made it home fine, back in time with what looked

like nothing to worry over. And it was then, alone, that Alice felt pure joy. Ahead of her in the falling ice she saw a light. She didn't identify it as a vehicle, a truck. It was the leader of those beasts, with a small, contained light hanging from its great neck. Look at it sway slowly in the cold night. It had come for Alice and Alice had not been afraid.

Why, at that precise time, when the truck sped her way, was Josh called out into the night to find her? Alice would never ask him. Yet whatever it was that had inexplicably compelled him was surely connected to the piece of her heart that would break clear through by the time the ice storm was over and Josh was gone.

It was Ronny in the truck that sped up and ran right into her, of course it was. Josh insisted it was not a mistake but how could Alice tell? That sore hip she'd had all winter—what did she know about mistake or purpose? After the disappearance of the light Alice's memory did not restart until there was nothing but the falling sky above her and a faint cry of a loon in the distance. She thought she had died. She thought even that it was some creature from another world that wrapped his arms around her and carried her home. It wasn't until he had set her in the bathtub that Alice knew it was Josh who saved her. He turned the water on and when it filled he slowly removed all her clothing. And even then he had done something for laughter, or at least she thought that's what the intent had been. In all his clothing he stepped into the bathtub with her, and laid his legs up the sides of her naked body. With her like that, Josh stayed until she was ready to fall asleep.

By morning the power had gone out, which meant the water, too. For one week that ice fell. Birds caught their feet in it and died that way, frozen to the ground. Trees were covered with a suffocating layer of ice more than an inch thick. Even people died, the old and frail without wood heat. Alice worried that Martha's family would not make it, but in this ice and sore as she was, Alice had no way of checking in on Martha. It took a week anyway for Alice to walk again. When she did finally emerge from bed and down the stairs, Josh opened his arms and took her in and she knew then that he was leaving.

Which he did, quick as that. During the storm, while she lay in bed, he had fixed her car for her and packed his own things. All that commotion, she thought he was cleaning up, rearranging. She thought he was just trying to keep warm. But there his truck was, loaded up in the dim purple morning. The sun had not yet risen when he walked out. It would take five days to drive back to the place he had come from.

How long did Alice sit alone in front of that woodstove? When the sun fell into her lap she went out. The storm had ended and those rays of light now transformed the frozen trees into fountains. Water poured down in great streams. Light bounced and caught until it was a kaleidoscope of a world. And there Alice stood within it, unexpectedly embraced.

In another day she walked the gully up to Martha's house. Without setting foot on the porch she could already tell that no one was inside. Not that anything looked different—the curtains had always been pulled, and there was rarely a car in the drive. Perhaps it was the silence spread round the place. Alice went onto the porch and knocked, then moved over to the window and knocked there, too. She should have been afraid. To die, yes, or to discover Martha's family dead. She imagined that, briefly, Ronny shooting his wife and then his children and finally shooting himself. Alice turned the doorknob and the door fell open.

Twice Alice called Martha's name, and then the children's, and finally she called for Ronny. "Ronny?" she said. "Ronny, I'm not afraid of you." When she had been through the entire house she went to the phone. Taped there beside it was a list, police and fire department, that sort of thing. If Martha had been allowed, Alice's number probably would have appeared there. The school number was there, though, and Alice called that up, found out that Christy and Jason were not in today. But school had been shut down for the length of the ice storm, so it was impossible to know how long they had been gone.

Ronny's work number was posted, too.

"He done gone," the man said.

"Sorry?"

"You find him you tell him to get his ass to work."

Alice hung up the telephone and walked slowly through the house, opening the curtains of every single window. A little light, that was better. Martha had made this place a comfortable home. Above the sink she kept a line of glass animal figurines, and at the end of it one rock, upon which someone had painted "Pet Rock." Throughout the house were more figurines, glass or porcelain, mostly of animals but some of ballerinas. By the couch was a table, and upon it, arranged perfectly straight, sat one TV guide and the remote control. There was a drawer in that table, and Alice opened it. Within was a small pink journal with a picture of a panda bear on the front. "My Diary," it read. Keeping it shut was a small metal lock attached to the front and back cover. Briefly Alice looked for the key, but ended up tearing the lock from the cover and opening the book. She had thought it would be Christy's—Alice had not considered that the diary would belong to Martha. From it a folded piece of paper fell to the floor. The map for seeing the ghost of the train—Martha had said she and her son had made that. It was drawn in crayon, and so detailed that Martha's and even Alice's house was marked. In the bottom left corner was a box labeled "Key": *Up to end of our road. Before road meets Perkins you turn in left, step over stone wall. Back way into woods, up and up and then you come to an edge you look down into a gully. Down there them old train tracks to run right into town. IMPORTANT: Full moon at midnight you see it!* And in the bottom right corner, *This detailed map by Jason and Martha Paquette (Missy Mom).*

Alice folded the map and tucked it into the back flap of the diary, but then reconsidered and put it into her own pocket. Then she flipped through the diary. The pages were predated from years back, but with a black marker Martha had crossed out each incorrect day of the week and replaced it with this year's correct one. On days she didn't write in the journal, Martha simply left the page—with the correct date—blank.

SATURDAY, MAY 2: *Macaroni and Cheese for dinner.*

MONDAY, SEPTEMBER 21: *Christy says she got a solo in the chorus! I says Christy I promise I will hear you sing your solo. I just can't believe it! I tell her that all my life I wants to sing a solo in the chorus! Can you believe it?*

Alice skipped ahead to when they had met. Here her own name appeared day after day. MONDAY, OCTOBER 19: *Talked to Alice today.*

TUESDAY, OCTOBER 20: *Alice my best friend says I am a funny person!*

WEDNESDAY, DECEMBER 16: *I been noticing my friend Alice's hands, she got Hill hands just like me. My mom always says you want to know a Hill you just look at her hands. Then I get to thinking and I know one thing, God forgive me for writing it down, us Hills and them Wickholms have a secret child from my disappeared cousin Jennifer Hill and their dead son, I don't know his name. That baby's been adopted and kept a big secret but then I get to looking at Alice's hands and I start thinking and I just have this feeling, forgive me if I am wrong, Alice, the secret is you!*

That entry Alice read twice, slowly, tracing her finger over the words. Hill hands. Of course it might not be true—that thought she had to reach out and grab, then coax back into her mind. But more present was this other one, the one where she could finally hear a sound that had always been playing. She reread the passage one final time, memorizing it, and then flipped forward, found the last entry. It was dated a week ago, when they had gone to the tracks. This page Martha had filled in with the smallest of letters, all the details of their plan and everything she thought might happen there. Alice skimmed the page and then flipped back one more day.

WEDNESDAY, JANUARY 13: *Finally I dared ask my best friend Alice why she limps and she says she got a bad hip and I ask her how she has a bad hip when she's not even thirty, does it run in the family? You know what? She says her husband pushed her straight down the stairs. Then she says no, it weren't on purpose. I says Alice, but then what? She admits something worse. She says when she fell she'd been carrying, but not no more. I says, does he love you? She says yes. Does he tell you he loves you? (How'd I know to ask that?!) And you know what, she says he ain't once said that. Alice! I say. Alice, that's your husband! She says "Martha" in that way she can say my name so I just slap her back and say it don't matter. He made a mistake, I say, that's the truth any way you look at it.*

Alice considered taking the journal with her. She even put it in her pocket, for she knew the police would show up eventually, and she didn't want them reading it. But still she opened the small drawer and put it back in, the lock affixed as much as it could be. She pushed the drawer shut with care. "Martha?" she called one more time. In the kitchen she went back to the phone. Martha at four a.m. needing salt. Martha at six needs milk, too.

I forgot to give Christy her cookies, you think you can run over to the school, just leave them in the office with the secretary?

"I don't like the way that woman treats you," Josh had said. Well, no matter. Now they both were gone. Alice called the police and said that her dear friend Martha had disappeared.

Alice lost count of days as she stayed on in Josh's lonely place. At the start, with buckets of steaming water she scrubbed the house clean. Hours she worked at it, with hardly a rest. At night she would crawl into bed and take the novel she was reading from under her pillow and in spite of herself she would feel something like satisfaction. Not that her heart wasn't broken clear through—just that in moments that solitude came to her so clean and arranged. Other times as she drove to the store or the library she would wonder what it might mean to drive straight off the cliff. She had no concept of how long she could last in this abandoned place, or of who might come to kick her out. Her savings were nearly half gone, and often she thought that she ought to pack her bags and head for her father's in Kettleborough. But something kept her waiting. That view of the mountains in the distance—winter had passed its peak by now but would have one more soft, deep snow before ending. In spring how green it all would be. When bills came she followed the same rule she always had—they were in Josh's name, she did not open them. Once in a while the telephone rang, and certainly a piece of Alice would wish wildly that Josh would be on the other end of the line. But then the person she allowed herself to expect was always Martha. Of course neither one ever called.

Josh did send one postcard, though. The picture—sent from him, so clearly a joke—showed a stretch of parking lot and a large industrial building. The words on the back could have been written to anyone, from anyone. Alice was not in the mood to laugh. She put it back in the mailbox and she waited for a ring of bare ground to form beneath the trees. This came first. The rest of the ground still had a hard, dirty layer of snow atop it. But here was earth, musty and thick. And pine needles, their contrasting greens a blessing upon the melting snow. Her bags were already packed. She phoned her father but could not bear to admit the truth. Instead she said that she and her husband would be traveling for the summer. I will be out of touch, she said. When Alice could take a handful of dirt from beneath any one of the trees in the flat yard and let it sift down through her fingers, she left that cold place on her own.

# The Village

## 1982

IN THAT FAR-OFF village that lay on the top of the cliff, visitors would be told only that whales could be seen. Scarcely anything else was ever said of the place. To the east, Newfoundland could be spotted in the distance, and the drop from the village to the ocean was at least eighty feet. The lush green forest and mountain looked the same as they had for hundreds of years, as did the cliff and ocean. The man who ran the campground would in time pass it on to his son, as his father and his father before that had done. Now the man was nearing seventy and with the tourists he kept his mouth shut most of the time.

"Whales," he said, and also, "Bundle of wood five dollars,"

or whatever the price might be that year, and "Don't move the picnic tables," and "Emergency brake please."

There wasn't much privacy there and each year the stretch of grass got more and more crowded, but the beauty of the cove, people came and loved it all the same.

In that place there lived only one outsider, and she never did say where she was from. She claimed her name was Cici, and people understood that she must have had some trouble. She's so beautiful, they would say. Why would she come here alone? She had arrived in the midst of her twenties, dressed in brighter clothing than anyone from around there wore. That was more than twenty years ago. Back then she had attempted to befriend people, she brought flowers on May Day and she picked apples from all the wild trees she could find and then she tracked down a press and invited the village over for a cider party. People showed up to these sorts of events because they were curious about her. Her earrings dangled down to her chin and for a necklace she wore an oyster shell large as a hand.

"Whales," she said when people asked her why she had come. "Whales, of course, why else do people come here?"

"She must be rich," they said to one another, and in comparison she certainly was. None of these people would move from the land their great-great-grandfathers had settled, not unless it was for a thing like marriage. But back then she really hadn't had much money, and nearly all she had saved—three thousand dollars—had been spent on the trailer that she would, in later years, convert to a real house. She had no car. Oscar had been coming back from the city when he picked her up on the road. He liked to think that if it had not been for him she would not have stayed, which certainly might have been true. Oscar was a little different from most people in the cove: thanks to his grandmother he had been to college, and now together he and Cici could talk about Rilke and Keats and the greater world.

Back then, Cici had volunteered at the schoolhouse, teaching the little children. They had never known an outsider before, and they giggled at the way her accent was so very different from their own, but still she was able to teach them to read smoothly and with pleasure. She let them sit on her lap, she braided the girls' hair, she laughed. The children loved her and she loved them and in time the head teacher retired and Cici took over.

Some days, the children wanted to go down to the beach. There they would lay dried seaweed on the sand and run back and forth over it and as the bells on the buoys echoed the children would shout, "The monsters are here, the monsters are here!" One day a girl began to talk about the van that had fallen over the ledge and now rested in the water.

"I don't know, maybe forever ago."

The girl said that the baby had died and the parents had left and now there was the ghost of the baby living in the van in their cove. That was why there were so many whales. They kept watch.

"It's true," the other children said. Their parents had told them the very same thing. Cici hadn't heard this version before.

"The baby didn't die down there," she said, and she took them away from the beach.

When Alice knocked on Cici's door, Cici was in her mid-forties. The girl would be twenty-four this fall, Cici knew.

"Yes?" Cici said shamelessly, her face revealing not an ounce of recognition. And Alice, too, revealed nothing. It was Sunday and the rain had finally quit and now sunlight poured into her small house so intensely that Cici had to grip the doorframe to keep herself from tipping over. That other life she had had.

Back in the days of Mike Shaw, when Alice was sixteen, she had asked her father for more details about this woman. He had let out a long breath, almost like a whistle, rubbed his rough hands together as though to gather warmth, and then walked to his closet and taken an old map from the top shelf. He spread it on his bed and pointed to an unmarked spot in the eastern reaches of Canada. The place he suspected she would be. *My wife*, he had said, and then, *your mother*. Alice had clung to that word, *mother*, but it wasn't until she drove away from Josh's empty house that she found the courage to keep heading north and east until she landed at this remote point. Because now, with scarcely anything left inside of her, how much more could she lose? She had meant to ask questions: *Did you love me? Why did you leave us?* And finally, *Am I really yours?* Instead she said only, "I'm sorry. The man at the campground told me to come here. He said you know something about whales."

That was true. Her shelves were lined with books about them; each time a family went south to the city she would send them with money to bring back one more book. She could say what kind of whale rose from the water when; she said she recognized each individual whale and knew how long it had been returning to the cove.

A foghorn sounded. That would be Oscar out on his boat, sending his ritual hello. Cici crossed the room, went to the porch, and gave a broad wave. When she turned back around, the girl was in the living room, looking at the walls. They were covered with paintings that Cici had collected over the years. Most were done by Oscar's sister, who painted brave, colorful pieces on oversized canvases. She hadn't had an ounce of training and for Cici this made the bravery of the paintings even stronger. The one the girl looked at now was Cici's favorite. It was of a whale but it had a block-like quality to it, a child could have painted it, and it was so large that it overtook nearly an entire wall. Cici suddenly knew she was going to vomit.

"I'm sorry," she said. "You'll have to go."

. . .

It was no wonder that the man at the campground would next tell Alice to track down Oscar. He was the one who liked to talk to outsiders. He'd had a wife once, long ago, who had come here from the city. Eventually she left with their daughter—he could admit that his own drinking had done it. But he had long since quit that. Cici had been in his life for more than twenty years now. He wanted to marry her but she would not, but he loved her and was happy all the same.

At the wharf Oscar told the girl that he would take her on the boat the following day. He did it because she was young and nice enough and because it wasn't often that someone had the courage to ask.

Also it might work out well for Oscar. He and Cici, after all these years, had had their first fight last month. It was over a vacation he wanted to take—he'd planned the whole two weeks, even paid ahead for some of it. They would go to the Bay of Fundy and then down to the city. They would eat French food and stay in hotels and they would be tourists and it would be grand. Cici had refused—she always refused, she would go nowhere—and Oscar had stormed out and now a month had gone by and neither of them had had the sense to apologize. Now with the girl Oscar could. Cici loved a visitor, so he could bring her over and the three of them would eat lobsters.

In the morning Oscar outfitted Alice in a yellow rain suit much too large for her and told her to expect to be sick, what with the waves and the stench of the bait. She said she wanted to see whales, that she had meant to be a scientist but had never done well enough in school. A camera hung from her neck and she said that she had also thought to be a photographer but had never been good enough at that, either. Just seeing them would be enough, she said. And maybe the library in her hometown might like to hang a few photos.

She did marvelously on the boat. Not once did she hang her head over the edge. She didn't complain and she didn't speak too much and she had a way of speaking to Oscar's teenage stern man that seemed to put him right at ease.

"I have a wet suit," Oscar heard her tell the boy. "I don't have the nerve to scuba dive but I'm going to snorkel. What are the chances of seeing a whale underwater?"

"Might see that old van," Oscar called to her from behind the wheel. "Old town legend. Gus at the campground best to tell it. Says a young couple parked there and he watched their van go over into the water. Says their baby was inside. That's why they disappeared. They stole his truck and it didn't turn up until two days later, down in the city. Now the whales keep watch over the baby, that's the story."

Alice looked out over the still blue water, waiting for a whale to appear. Her father had told her of this place, and he was right—the beauty, she had seen nothing like it. But there was something else, too. The danger of the cliff, it may have been that. The poverty perhaps. Something here scared her. When she stood at the edge of the cliff in the night she became afraid not that she would fall over the ledge but that she might jump.

"Got lobsters," Oscar said later, when she was back at the campground. It was just about dinnertime and she was going to heat a can of beans by the fire but here he was, wanting to take her for dinner. She got in his truck.


When Cici opened the door she was already a bit drunk. She embraced Oscar and whispered something in his ear and then she put her hands on Alice's cheeks and asked, "Where are you from?"

"Kettleborough," Alice said, as though that was a place people would know.

"Yes, yes you are," Cici said back.

They ate lobsters and listened to Alice talk about the lake where she had grown up, the courses she had taken in college. Before the meal was through, Cici said, "And your father? Tell me how your father is." Alice went still at that, and in a moment Cici just excused herself and went to the bedroom, closed the door.

"I've never seen her like this," Oscar said. "I'm sorry." To try to keep the conversation going, he told her again that maybe she'd see that van underwater. Maybe a whale lived in it, he announced foolishly.


Cici, in her bedroom and a little drunk but not near so bad as Oscar and Alice thought, heard that. She lay on her quilt with her arms spread wide. She had brought this quilt from home— the one belonging that stretched back into the space of her previous life. A woman out on Bear Island had sewn it for her when she'd first married, and she had loved it for the colors, which matched the lake. She turned over and dug her nose into the blanket as though there would be an old lake smell trapped in there from more than two decades ago. The love she'd had then, she thought of how desperate and vital it had been. The entire time she and Paul had been together, people had always mistaken them for honeymooners. She'd been pretty then, she knew that, pretty and self-assured, and he could have walked right out from a movie screen.

When she woke up it was still the dark of morning and Oscar was asleep beside her in all his clothes. He wouldn't go out on the boat today. Cici started a fire and put a saucepan of coffee grounds and water atop it. When Oscar rose he stood in the picture window for a long while. When he turned to her she knew he was angry. He'd always known there was something in her past that sent her away—a woman wouldn't come here alone without that. He had accepted it. He didn't tell her everything, either. But there had been rumors about her—Gus at the campground started them way back. He said she was the one who had killed her own baby. That circulated right around until Oscar put a stop to it without Cici's ever knowing a word had been said.

"Ain't her name, look right there in your book," Oscar had told Gus.

"Changed it, maybe she has," Gus had said.

Back then Oscar had understood that the town wanted her to be some criminal, at least just a little bit they wanted that, for it would provide excitement and years of storytelling. But Gus was wrong, Oscar had been sure of it, and on top of that Oscar had already begun to fall in love with her.

"I'll go away," Cici said now. "Anywhere you like." On a trip with him is what she meant, but she knew it didn't come out that way. Oscar left. He had intended to drive home but from the top of the cliff he could see Alice down there in her wet suit, a mask on her forehead and a snorkel hanging next to her mouth. She looked helpless and it would be cruel and even dangerous to let her go out there without someone watching. He drove down to the beach.

"I've practiced plenty," she said.

"Who knows what's down there."

"I know," she said. It wasn't said in agreement. It was a claim she was making.

The lupines were out in full bloom, and before she went into the water she walked up the hill and took one careful photograph of the flowers. This morning, just when the light had begun to spread across the cliff, she'd heard a rustle and peered outside her tent. Cici, on her tiptoes. The woman had held her breath as she opened Alice's car door and placed something inside. She closed the door, turned, and then turned back, opened the door again. From her view in the tent, Alice could see only that Cici went to the car twice; she couldn't tell that all Cici had done was move the envelope from the seat to the dashboard and then back to the seat. When the car door was closed once more, Alice expected her to walk off again, but instead she approached the tent. Alice froze in her upright position, unsure as to whether Cici could see in or not. Cici froze, too, and Alice felt certain that for a moment their eyes locked in that dim morning light that was dimmer still with the screen of the tent between them. Neither said a word. Cici left. When Alice was sure that Cici would be out of sight, she crawled out of the tent to see what was there. She had expected a letter, an explanation. An apology. Instead there was a deed for a cabin and a small plot of land out on an island on the lake, along with an old map and a scribbled note: *Left to you by a Kettleborough woman named Signe.* For a moment the coldness of the exchange shocked Alice, and her instinct was to chase Cici up the road and return the envelope to her. But then neither of them had ever dared speak bluntly to each other; Alice had made her attempt and now Cici had made her own. She left the envelope on the seat and returned to her tent until the sun was high.

Now, with flippers on her feet, Alice made her way into the frigid water. Her steps were awkward, but still there was no hesitation in them, though in truth she had not practiced, not in the ocean. She had practiced plenty in the lake, but that had been years ago, and anyway there was a current here and the water was so cold and there was that terror, too, this ocean so vast and the life in it unknown. Underwater, darkness occupied most of her sight, with only an occasional beam of light. She kept the edge of the cove in view but did not go too close to it, in case a wave should change direction and sweep against the side of the rock rather than the shore. The seaweed was tall and she had the sense that she was drifting atop a forest canopy. There were no fish, none that she saw. When the light glinted she knew she had found the van. It was where she had imagined it to be. She came up and held tight to a rock, lifted her mask from her face and looked to shore. It wasn't but twenty feet away. She had worn a life jacket but now she removed it and hitched it with its strap to a tangle of seaweed on the rock. She took a deep breath and plunged herself under.

The van still stood straight up, as though it had grown out from the seafloor and longed for light. Without knowing what she was looking at she might have known only that a large hunk of rusted metal lay beneath the water. The water down there was gentle, and in it one open door swayed lightly back and forth. So this was what she had come in search of. Not a thin, cold, unknowable woman whose features would never match her own, but the proof, drowned and rusted, that she herself had impossibly clung to life. That no matter how little she felt she belonged in this world, she had known, in her infant self, how to reemerge into it.

"Any whales?" Oscar asked when Alice returned.

Alice was dripping and cold and in her hands she held her life jacket, snorkel and mask, and flippers. Wet and burdened as she was, she looked nothing but pathetic.

"The baby didn't die and the van's still there," she said. "You can tell your Clara that."


Back home, the woman who had become Cici put water on for tea. She took out her stack of records but decided instead on silence. In the bottom of her underwear drawer she had a picture. She locked the doors of her place and took that picture out. Sun poured in. It had been like that then; all of her memories of that time were filled with light plunged down for their small family alone. And that had been good, full, and surely would have grown. But now what was she to do? She could not ever say that when that great beast with barnacles on its back rose from the depths she had chosen to leave her family and instead join with that animal in a flight far above all that her life had ever been or would be. But that is what she had done. It might not have been a mistake.

# The Island

## 1982

ALICE RECEIVED HER first letter in early spring. It wasn't expected. The last stretches of ice had vanished from the lake just days ago. In her time so far on the island, Alice had performed this ritual of checking mail every day. It began at her cabin. She would sit on her porch in the late hours of morning, the spread of empty lake before her, and when the mail boat drifted across the horizon like a slow, sure animal, she would slip her shoes on and begin her short run to the mail dock. When she arrived, Kenneth, the mailman, would just be docking his boat. His job was to deliver mail to all the islands. Here, though no one ever got mail, there stood a spread of boxes, one for each summerhouse that speckled the shore of Bear Island. Until today, the mail itself had never been Alice's purpose, though she had imagined, more than once, that Josh had tracked her down and sent her a letter. Not that she would take him back—she felt sure she would not. Since she came to the island, the mornings of immobility, those days when she felt she could sleep for a hundred years, had vanished. Yet there was something she felt she still wanted from him. It had scarcely been two months since she had left that cold place, and though she felt impossibly wiser now, some part of her wanted to know that in her days in the north, distant though it all seemed now, she had not been a fool. That he had loved her then—a small piece of her still wanted and would always want to know that. But of course such reassurance would never come, and during these long days on the island it simply felt good to have a ritual, and a person to greet each day. Now, as she withdrew her letter, Kenneth the Federal Agent—as he liked to call himself—peered over her shoulder.

"Bet I know that handwriting," he said. "But that ain't for a Federal Agent to be saying."

Alice placed the worn envelope in her back pocket and flushed. Kenneth, that's who she imagined had written it. A bit of a gift. He untied his boat and was off.

*Door to your cabin says Wickholm Ice Cream & Candy. Heavy door with a mail slot. So I'm no stranger. Guessing you know the Wickholms since you're out there at Signe's place. Malcolm Wickholm been like family to me, but he don't know about the cabin far as I know. No one but Signe knew, don't know why. Signe wanted the cabin fixed up and she hired me to do it, five years back, maybe a few more. Simon Wentworth is my name.*

*Anyway I got out there and the place had been destroyed, rotted right through and the roof sunken in with snow, so I cleared it all away and fixed up another. Something you might like to know, your cabin is an old chicken coop. I went over there to the Phillipses' farm and I see the coop they're all set to burn and I buy the thing. Jack that thing right up, put it on runners, tow that place out right over the water. Fixed it up. Now you's living in an old chicken coop.*

*I ain't on the island now. Up north working on an old barn. Don't know what you like, but it's something. Old notched beams. Maybe I'm speaking down to you by saying there ain't a nail in the place.*

*I seen you fixing up that cabin, that's all. I got a place out there inland so I seen what you done and Patty Jean told me who you were, and once I heard your name I realized I remember you from school, you were a few grades younger than me. All I'm saying is the thing was liable to fall into the ground. Now you're there and you painted the porch. Raise the flag in the morning. Flag ain't my kind of fixing but looks nice in the wind all the same.*

*Also I seen you read. Signe's books are good but if you want something else you go inside your cabin. Top shelf behind the door, find an old property map all rolled up. Find Wentworth easy. Only place inland on the island. Combination 5731. Old ice cream store number, Malcolm's store. Don't know why I chose it but I did. You go right in. Don't need to check no books out. If there's food eat it. Be on the island soon.*

As far as Alice knew, the only other living soul on the island was Patty Jean. That woman lived just one cove down from Alice, and Alice had made something of a ritual of visiting her, too, but only in the evenings. That was because she didn't want to intrude. "How I love my lonely days," Patty Jean had said once, when Alice asked her how she kept herself busy. She was an old woman, her husband gone and her daughter off with her own life somewhere. In winters, Patty Jean lived in an apartment in New York City, but each spring, as soon as the ice cleared enough for passage, she found herself a ride out to her island house, and there she stayed until the freeze began in fall. On her walls hung framed notes from her late husband, things written on scraps of paper and even napkins. *Gone to pick mushrooms, don't eat all my dinner up. Me and the dog and the cat love you, and we're all sorry for being cranky.* Also she kept framed photos of herself, black and white, alone or with a baby on her lap. In these photos she sat bold and so serene. Evenings, Alice would sit with her on the screened porch, and together they would listen for loons while they cut squares for the quilts Patty Jean sewed.

With Patty Jean sharing this strip of land Alice had never before been afraid out here, but now she looked behind herself wondering what man might be lurking in the woods. She put the letter into her pocket and heated that great big, freshly seasoned pan over the fire. The entire lake was dark now. A deep wind had set in and the whitecaps were picking up speed. She wrapped a shawl around her shoulders and peeled her garlic and threw whole cloves into the hot oil, and as it sizzled she kept her vision fixed on the waves, and it wasn't long until her thoughts boiled down to become nothing at all. Nothing but her cabin soaring across the water, this Simon at the bow as though he were aboard a great ship.

*Dear Simon,*

*I have received your letter, what a special gift. Also I have found my way up to your cabin. I must say that it was an offer I did not originally intend to accept, yet with all the free time on this island it simply became too tempting a journey. And as you say, I suppose we two are not strangers, though I am afraid I do not remember you from school; sometimes I marvel at how I was able to keep so to myself in a town as small as ours. Anyway, how grateful I am for your books, as I have recently committed myself to the Classics.*

*Your cabin is something—so well thought out, such reasonable, usable space. And insulated! Do you stay on through winter? These cold nights I often start a fire in my small woodstove, but the heat vanishes straight through the thin walls.*

*Save for Patty Jean I have not yet seen a soul out here. Except of course Kenneth, the mailman. It was he who first delivered me to the island—though he said it was against the law to carry a passenger aboard the federal mail boat, and insisted I keep the small journey a secret. I'm confident that my secret is safe with you. When were you here? Why didn't you introduce yourself? Know that incurable shyness is certainly something I understand. I often curse myself for being incurably shy.*

*I look forward to meeting you out here on Bear, Mr. Simon Wentworth.*

With her first letter written from the island, Alice walked early to the mail dock and waited for Kenneth. When his boat arrived she headed to the end of the dock and caught the line he tossed to her. After she'd tied the stern of the boat up, and Kenneth had come off to tie the bow, she walked to him and waved her letter his way.

"Oh, no, missy," Kenneth said. "That ain't the law. Things is different on this here lake." Kenneth went to the side of the mail boat and released a latch, pulled forth a narrow set of stairs just long enough to hit the dock, and held out his hand for Alice.

"It's the law, missy," he said. Alice took his hand and he led her up the stairs, onto the mail boat.

"Thought no one was allowed on," she said.

"Women," Kenneth mumbled, and then, "Ain't no one allowed a *ride*." Here he winked at her. "Dropping outgoing mail into the box a whole other matter altogether." He released her hand, pointed to the blue box that was anchored to the floor of the boat, and then shaded his eyes. "Privacy," he said, "is a very important part of a Federal Agent's responsibilities."

"Don't you know he just makes up every single one of those rules," Patty Jean would tell Alice later. "It was thanks to him I quit sending mail long ago." But still, Alice would continue to feel quite right about every part of the official island process. The wasted effort she rather enjoyed.

*Cabin's insulated right up, good to stay the winter, though I ain't never done that. You want yours warmer? I'd say we could do something easy. Fix the roof up first thing in order. Insulating a chicken coop ain't the brightest thing I ever heard of, but I seen stupider things done. What I'm saying is I'll do it if you want. Won't cost much and besides I got some stuff we can use.*

*Where you been these last years? Be on the island soon.*

*Dear Simon,*

*I daresay this island is the most beautiful corner of the world I ever did know. Summer has arrived, I swim each day, and Patty Jean has taught me how to hunt for, pick, and dry some edible wild mushrooms. It frightens me a bit, to eat the little things, but Patty Jean assures me that she is an expert and that life is too short to miss out upon black chanterelles.*

*You asked where it is I have come here from. Most recently I was up north of the mountains. I had some difficult times there.*

*Inheriting this cabin was a pure surprise and blessing. At the time, I had nowhere to go. My first and in truth my only thought was to go into the lake. That sounds strange and terrifying, but I do find it astonishing that after such a thought I should land in this blessed place. It is difficult to describe. The simplest version is to say that I was raised by my father; my mother left us when I was an infant. Recently I drove northward and tracked her down in the place my father said she would be. She lives in a small village on the eastern tip of the continent, in Canada. While I was there she left an envelope on the seat of my car. In it were the details of this place, my inheritance. It seems that in the year I was born, this Signe you speak of gave my mother the deed to this cabin and land, with the instructions that I should have it when I was old enough. I do wonder what would have happened had I never showed up. Would the papers have just sat there in a drawer? And as for this place? Anyway, I'm afraid that I never knew Signe, and am yet unsure of my relation to her. I also do not know the Wickholms—of course, I know who they are, but I have never had an occasion to meet them, though I am now inclined to believe that we too share a strong connection. Oh, it is all still so confusing to me! Suffice it to say that I am trying to figure it all out, and in the meantime there isn't a place in the world where I would rather be.*

*Being from Kettleborough, you must know the story of the Witches. Patty Jean has just retold it to me. Ida of the Witches! Growing up, my father told me that story many times. He would joke that that woman had been my ancestor. But aren't those only stories? Now, standing on shore and looking out to those black rocks—how like witch hats they do look—I can so clearly imagine a woman dropping within to have those rocks rise up in her place. Yesterday I found the spot marked "Witches" on the map, and I walked the perimeter of the island until I came to the place nearest to them. I stood there on shore for some time and imagined myself the woman of the story. How strange, I know. But it seemed a wonder to me that my feet were planted so closely to the last solid spot that such a legend stood. I truly felt rooted there. It was as though the rocks called out to me. I stared and stared while the time passed. And time did pass—it was nearly dusk when I came to. I walked back to my cabin then, thinking all the while of this floating strip of land, this great expanse of lake, and those great rocks. It all fills me with a pure steadiness, Simon. Is it strange to say I feel I have come home? This island holds me up in some real way.*

*I look forward to your arrival. Solitude is wonderful but now and again quite lonely. How does Patty Jean make it out here so long alone? Ghosts, that is what she tells me! Perhaps, but I think I prefer the living.*

*Be well, dear Simon.*

*P.S. I would love to fix this place up some more. Please do let me know the details.*

*Live alone and maybe I already told you but I have a dog. Yesterday maybe 5 in the morning I throw the tennis ball for him, throw it way out into the woods. He runs off, gone all day. Evening I start to call him, hear him bark back at me so I don't worry none. Arthur. I let him do what he wants. But I wondered, because that dog likes to eat, and usually he shows up for dinner real early. Round 9 o'clock I get ready for bed and the slobbering beast runs in through the screen door wagging his tail so hard he knocks a glass of water off the table and it breaks. I look at him and that son of a bitch has the ball in his mouth, no shit. Out there looking for it all day. I couldn't believe it.*

*I got insulation for you. Whole one-ton truck full of it. I'll get out there soon. We'll fix your place up good enough to winter the island.*

*Dog is good but it will be nice to have some company out there.*

*Dear Simon,*

*Like clockwork, each morning I wake just a moment before sunrise and open my eyes. Why I wake at this time each morning I do not know, yet my best guess is that it is in that moment before sunrise that the lake is entirely quieted. I sleep in the front room, in the bed closest the window, so when I open my eyes, instantly my vision is cast upon the water. And at that moment it is nothing but a plate of glass with stars that shine up from within it. From star to star, how I could skip across the lake.*

*Winter the island! I admit I have dreamed of it. Is it truly possible? I understand that people have not lived year round out here for ages, yet I'm inclined to believe that it could be done without too much trouble. Your cabin has a good clearing in front of it—perhaps we could plant a garden, grow enough to store through winter. Oh, my imagination runs wild! Yet I must control it, for to winter the island in my old place would certainly lead to death.*

*Though perhaps you will arrive soon to help me fix it up? Yet now comes a time when I have to ask something difficult. It may prove to be a mistake. However, I have recently and severely been hurt by love. I came to this island to be alone. Yet here you are (in letters, at least!) and I cannot help but respond. What I mean to say is that if you intend to make a serious attempt at love with me, then we ought to continue. Yet if you consider yourself in any way the sort of man whom a woman might do best to avoid, then I would ask that you please back away from me now. I know that sounds quite harsh, but there it is. It is my one request.*

*Be well, dear Simon.*

*I know I ain't out there yet. I been busy with work. Also I been meaning to tell you that I am fat and I ain't never had a girlfriend. But I been getting to thinking about you a lot these days in truth.*

*Anyway, once I get out there, you like what you see, I got another idea. All my life I wanted to winter the island, so I figure we could just do that in my place. If yours ain't done is all I mean.*

It was Tasha, Kenneth's woman, who convinced Simon to write this letter—a *love letter,* she called it. Simon lived with Kenneth and Tasha, and in Tasha's opinion Simon was her very best friend.

"I bet Simon knows how to love a woman the right way," she told Kenneth, after the letter was mailed. To this Kenneth smacked her ass and made a show of unhooking his belt.

"I'll show you the right way," he said.

Flowers, letters, a birthday cake—these were the things Tasha had meant. "I just might leave you," she said. Since they were fourteen years old the two of them had been together. "We can't even have kids." It was true, she had tried. Yet to this Kenneth winked, told her the problem with that wasn't in his *little swimmers.* "It's probably all them things you did to me when I was too young to be doing them," she said. Kenneth slapped her ass one more time.

Simon had wanted Tasha to read his love letter, but she had insisted that that was a private matter. So she didn't know what he had written. Winter the island? She would have said that was fast moves. She would have suggested dinner, a movie. Instead she imagined the letter he had mailed and she said, "Simon will make a good man to some woman." In response Kenneth walked up the stairs, lay down fully clothed upon the bed, and stayed there until morning.

At her cabin, Alice dropped her clothes onto the beach and put her hand to her belly. Slowly she walked into the lake until the water covered her knees. The water was so calm that if she squinted, she could barely perceive the line where the lake ended and the sky began. Though it was full into summer nothing passed before her, no sailboat or motorboat or canoe, no loon, either, or even a gust of wind. The sun was at her back and she turned into it, faced the island. Her cabin sat low, sunken in the center and a shade browner than the sand. Pale green moss gleamed atop the roof. The birch tree grew dangerously close. She dropped herself backward into the water and floated there, looking only at the sky. She had started a fire on shore, and now smoke came out to drift above her. Alice kicked and turned over, swam with her eyes open. She could see down to the floor of the lake, and every so often the shine of a fish caught her vision and then vanished. *Getting to thinking about you a lot these days in truth.* First Alice pictured those months of snow on the island. They'd find old wooden skis, and together she and Simon would carve trails around the island, down the old stone sheep run, across the lake. How they would return to tea and blankets and love. How they'd keep warm. She saw the water spring, surrounded in snow but still flowing upward. Then those months in between the ice and thaw. Alice and Simon, the only people on the island, no way on and no way off. The bread she'd bake. The walks as the fallen leaves gave over to brown or the naked trees began to sprout. And then the life, the children. A life that people live. Alice swam to shore. Her spot on the island was cast in shadow now, and she shivered naked by the fire.

*Dear Simon,*

*Mornings, this small place fully bathed in sun, I feel there isn't a spot farther east that a person can get. And this feeling comforts me, as though it was something I had for years unknowingly searched for.*

*Patty Jean is teaching me to sew a quilt. Read, swim, walk, cook, sew, what a simple life it is out here.*

*Oh, Simon, I am glad to hear you think of me often, as I think of you. Your invitation to winter with you came as quite a shock, yet as Patty Jean has said to me more than once, life is too short. Yes is my answer. Yes, dear Simon, what have we got to lose?*

"Lots of letters to Simie," Kenneth said. They were on the mail dock, Alice holding one end of the envelope, Kenneth the other. Lately he had taken to breaking his own rule by not lowering the steps for her to walk aboard, but rather holding out his hand for the letters.

"Lots of letters to him," Kenneth repeated. He slipped the letter from her grip and dropped it into his breast pocket. Then he tucked his thumbs into his belt loops and tipped back on his heels. "You met him?" he asked. Alice didn't know that Kenneth knew the answer. She didn't know Kettleborough anymore, couldn't know that Simon and Kenneth were friends and even that they lived together. Nor did she know that Kenneth's own damn woman kept saying that Simon knew how to love a woman. Bullshit. Alice's ignorance pleased Kenneth greatly. "Simie?" he continued. "Suppose you two go way back?" Now he was at the bowline, jerking the boat in closer, thrusting his hips forward with each pull. The movement was obscene.

"Yes," Alice said sternly. "Way back." Kenneth was her friend. She liked meeting Kenneth on the mail dock. So perhaps now she misunderstood.

"I bet you do," Kenneth said with a wink. Quickly he ran his tongue across his upper lip. "Well." He removed the letter from his pocket, smelled it. "Well then. You can bet this letter will get straightaway where it needs to go."

This Alice had never doubted. But now. No. Surely her letters got where they needed to go. "Kenneth," Alice said. She didn't know what else to say.

Kenneth winked. "Do I know Simon?" he asked. "That what you mean? Sure as hell I knows Simon." He tapped the letter against his arm in even intervals. "I knows he ain't where you sending these letters."

"Of course," she said. "People keep PO boxes, that's all. You ought to know that. They keep the boxes and they don't live there, they just keep them and gather their mail when they want." Alice spoke quickly. She had begun to sweat.

"That's a lot of mail gathering," Kenneth said. He came in closer to her. The sun was hot upon them and she could smell his stale coffee breath. The dock became narrow and Alice dizzy. Her hand went out to grab hold of the post for balance.

"Kenneth," she said. He had been her friend. What had come over him? Jealous, she thought suddenly. Federal Agent Kenneth must have developed a little crush on me. "Kenneth," she said, softly.

"Whoa there," Kenneth said. He held his arms out to her, a horse he meant to calm. Then he went to the stern line, untied it. "You alls is falling in love is how I take it," he said as he climbed on board, that letter now sticking out from his back pocket. He started the engine. That sentence, it had come out of his mouth by surprise. Falling in love, he thought as he lowered the throttle. If I could make Tash fall in love with me once more. The bow reared and then planed. The letter was still in his pocket, and Kenneth's hand went to it. Pulled it out. It was a sunny, warm day. Summer would soon be over. Once out in the middle of the lake, Kenneth slowed the boat again, cut the engine. He sat down in the stern, put his feet up. The letter was now on his lap. A wind could have come through, blown it into the lake. But that didn't happen. Instead, the letter waited on his lap while he rested both hands behind his head and then lowered one. Simon knows how to make a woman love him. Bullshit. He lowered his other hand. Carefully he opened the letter, read it quickly, trembling. Of course it couldn't be mailed now, not after it had been opened. In a rush Kenneth tucked it into his lunch bag. It wasn't something he meant to do, opening it, reading it, taking it home with him. This thought Kenneth repeated like a prayer in the days to come. Yet after that first letter, Kenneth couldn't bear to not open the next. Addiction, that's what he might have called it.

*Dear Simon,*

*Blueberries have come and gone, but I have removed the screens from the back windows of the cabin and used them to dry most of what I picked. One screen toppled over when a wind came across the island. I thought of letting the berries go to waste, but I had the time. I picked them out from the sand one by one, and set them back to drying.*

*I have gone to your cabin quite a bit recently. Just looking around, imagining our life. I have no fears of it, and it is a wonderful feeling.*

*Kenneth has been kind enough to me these past months to bring out the groceries I need now and again, and I am using that opportunity to stock up, though I know that you, too, are certainly thinking of and preparing for our journey together. I have not told Kenneth, however, of what we plan. I do not know why, but I have not told Patty Jean, either. It just seems such a precious occurrence, and one I want to savor for a bit. Is that strange?*

*I imagine we have enough rice to last, and also plenty of beans and oatmeal. I hope you will enjoy what I cook!*

*Dear Simon,*

*It has been perhaps a month since I last received a letter, yet how many I have written. August is nearly ended. If you would like to cancel our arrangement, that is no problem. If you are nervous to meet me, please cast your nerves aside. What can the trouble be? In the least, Simon, please send me a note to say you have received mine.*

Spread before Alice and Patty Jean were reels of fabric—together they were at work on Alice's first quilt. Choosing fabric had been the hardest part. Alice would pick one pattern of blues and greens, try to match five more to it, but of course the colors were different and no two patterns ever matched entirely, so she'd put it all back and begin again.

"Just choose any damn thing," Patty Jean had said after an hour or so. Then she had swept her fingers across the wall of fabric, tapped and pulled different notes until she had a fine collection on the table. That had been weeks ago. Now, at the table, the two were pinning squares. In the time it took Alice to attach one square to another, Patty Jean had already pinned ten squares together. Alice pushed a pin through and pricked her finger. One minuscule drop of blood emerged. The wind picked up, and a mile or so out from shore a sailboat capsized. "I made a quilt for one man," Patty Jean said as she rocked. They were on the screened-in porch. Loons called back and forth from one cove to another. "Old Mr. Wentworth. Bastard." She laughed a high, thick laugh, and a loon called as though back to her alone. "I shouldn't speak ill of the dead. Bastard, though, and he knows it."

"Well," Alice said.

"You'll know young Simon," Patty Jean said now. "You've met him already? I told him to go over there and introduce himself.

But then I probably scared him. I keep telling him you'll make a good woman for him! He didn't come see you? It was just last week he was out here. He's a handsome one, too. A bit fat, but handsome. He'll shape right up. Lonely is all." Patty Jean had run out of squares, and now she stood. She flipped a reel of fabric as she spoke, laid a fresh yard out across the table. "He should have gone to see you. I looked at him and I said, Simon! Is that you? He'd cleaned himself right up, looked right happy. Course he had that girl with him. Kenneth's girl. You know, I ought to watch my mouth. I leaned right in, whispered, Simon, you leave this pretty young thing." Rather than walking to the spring, Patty Jean drank straight from the lake, always had. Now she patted the backs of her legs, reached for her mug of silty water, and sat down. "I don't like a girl who dyes her hair so blond and pulls out all her eyebrows. I said, Simon, you go get that Alice. Boy did that make him go red. You didn't see him? He didn't come down to you?"

This time, when Alice pricked her finger, it bled more. Yet she pretended it hadn't happened and continued pinning squares, a small dot of blood on each square she touched.

"You were right out there on the beach. I don't know why they didn't go meet you."

"No matter," Alice said, and undid the square she had just pinned. She would not let herself be made a fool.


*Dear Simon,*

*I shall interpret your silence as a wish to remain alone. That is okay. Please know that I continue to cherish the company your existence has given me in these months of mine on the island. I think of you often, and wish you well always.*

Briefly, Alice had thought of going up to Simon's cabin. She saw herself ransacking the place, finding letters to other women, from other women. His books she would throw to the ground. She could break a bag of flour over them and even break a window. But no, Alice would not do that. Yet she had written a number of drafts of this last letter. The first the cruelest and the rest less and less cruel until she finally sounded like the person she wanted to be. She would not go to his place again. She would not linger or wish. When she finished the kind letter she put it in an envelope and addressed it, sealed it. Alice was sitting on the porch, the early afternoon sun fully upon her, and when she finally squinted across the lake she was shocked to see that barge-like boat anchored not far in front of her property. She recognized the boat, the *Lawrence*, used to deliver building supplies to the islands. Wearing only her swimsuit and not feeling shy for it, Alice stood and waved. Yet quickly she realized that the driver had already rowed his way to shore and tied his rowboat. Now he stood on her rotting dock.

"Hello," she called down the beach, her hand shading the sun.

"Ayup," he called back up. He stretched his arms high above his head. A slice of his dark skin was revealed below the waist. Oh, she thought quickly and with a surge. Oh, here he is. That woman, that had been a sister. A cousin. Nothing like what Patty Jean had said. Here Simon is. Just a little shy. Not so heavy and sloppy, not so much at all.

"Simie up there says you needs some firewood," the man said.

Alice realized her mistake and cleared her throat.

"Gots to unload the son of a bitch," he said, and nodded toward the *Lawrence*.

"All right, then."

Alice stayed on the porch and the man stayed there on the low dock. He took his shirt off, his skin gleaming brown. From

his pants pocket he withdrew a pouch of tobacco, rolled a cigarette. He smoked slowly and with ease, and after a while he held
the cigarette with the corner of his mouth as he stretched his
arms upward once more.

"None too ugly here," he said.

Alice nodded, moved from the porch to the beach. "The
wood?" she asked.

"Oh sure," he said, *oh showa*. He dipped his cigarette into the
water and walked off the dock to the fire pit, threw the paper
and tobacco remains onto the black wood. Then from his pocket
he pulled a small bundle and held it toward Alice. "Mind?" he
asked. His shoulders were broad and thin and he was quiet but
not the least bit awkward.

"No, no," she said, though she didn't know until the wind
blew her way that what he was doing in the cup of his hands was
smoking some marijuana. When he finished, the man folded his
body over and unlaced his wet leather boots. Then he stepped
out of them and stretched his arms upward again, far above his
head. His ribs showed clearly and he was majestic, there in the
sun and half naked.

"What was it that Simon said?" Alice dared.

"His woman out here needs some wood."

"His woman?"

"Alice?"

"Yes."

"Mind?" he said again, and again she told him she did not.
Slowly he unhooked his leather belt and dropped his pants. He
wore underwear—this caught her somehow by surprise. In this
underwear he walked to the lip of the water, then remembered
his socks. These he took off and stepped toward the water again,
yet again retreated. Here he dropped his last bit of clothing from
his thin body. That last bit of skin, untouched by the sun, shone

starkly like snow against the rest. With grace the man dove into the lake. When he began to swim she watched his body through a layer of water. Above the rocks he glided until he had swum beyond her view. When he had been underwater and out of her sight for some time, a flash of fear moved across Alice's chest. But in a moment he emerged only to suck in another breath and continue.

His name was Isaac and before they slept together Alice cooked him dinner. They talked of Kettleborough and the lake but their talk was not much. Mostly they sat in silence by the fire, and when the sun had gone down and both of them knew he would neither unload the wood nor leave, he reached without hesitation across the sand to her body. In years to come, he would remain a gentle, dear friend to Alice, nothing more. Yet now they slept together without shame. Later, sometime in the early hours of morning, when he rose and ran a hand swiftly over her hair and then pulled his clothing on, Alice sat up and looked straight at him.

"I don't need the wood," she said. "Maybe Simon needs it but I do not. I am leaving the island before summer's end. And I don't even know who Simon is, so you do what you want."

# Polite

## 1982

I NEVER WANTED my son to return home. Karl could have returned; in fact he could have remained in Kettleborough all his life and I would not have had a single misgiving, for he was a simple and happy being and had he lived, he would have done well to take over his father's business. Not Malcolm.

He did go to Europe for a time, you know. My Malcolm took a room in an aging woman's flat; he bought her groceries and cooked her meals. It was from this woman that he bought an opal ring, too—he was in Paris, and he had fallen in love with a French girl. Those days of my son's must have been the happiest and most carefree of his life. That dear girl, Francesca was her name, came from the countryside and when a letter arrived saying that he would marry her, I was so thrilled that I did not even tell Otto, for I worried that he would have some trouble with it. We had not met her, after all, and there was no invitation to the ceremony included. That was the sort of thing Otto would have gotten worked up about, and I knew his behavior could ruin the happy time.

Anyhow, it wasn't long after he left that girl that he returned home. Thankfully he didn't leave her at the altar. Back then he did tell me once that he had just driven off without a word in the middle of the night. Now he says that nothing such as that happened, and that I must have dreamed it. Still, I often think of that poor girl spending her life wondering whatever became of the American man who had been the love of her life.

After that he went west, and it was in California that he had the accident. He had read a book about the logging industry out in Oregon and he had been so moved by it that he thought it a life he ought to live, so he had found a friend and together they began their drive through the night. Malcolm had been driving when the car tumbled off the road. They'd been high on a cliff overlooking the ocean, and the nurse told me that when he first came to he said he had seen the lake when he crashed. She didn't understand what this meant—of course she wouldn't—but I knew.

I always hoped that you, too, would find some solace in the lake, dear Alice.

The truth is that I am getting older than most people know. Yesterday after washing the dishes I turned the garbage disposal on and after about twenty seconds I wanted to turn it back off but I could not remember how to do it. It is just a switch beneath the kitchen sink, and to turn it on is really no different than to turn it off, but I could not remember. I ran around the house looking for the place while that machine ground away, and after ten minutes I calmed myself down and breathed deeply and then I saw it. After that terrible episode I sat down in my chair and closed my eyes and when Otto returned home he wanted to know what the problem was but of course I could not tell him. He is a gentle old man, gentler and gentler as the days go on, and he loves me so, and to worry over my well-being is not something I imagine him capable of doing at this stage in life. We had a difficult time of it in the early years, but as I look back I can say with certainty that we shared a wonderful marriage. Now the years have caught up to him, too; he nods off in the day and he has had three falls so far. One was outside in the drive and we had to call an ambulance.

Caring for Otto, playing the hymns for him, looking after my plants, these are the things that keep me busy but it is not busy enough. I have a lot of time to sit and think, and more often than not my thoughts go to you.

Your father had a lovely girlfriend, you know. Of course that would be your mother. Jennifer Hill was her name and she was so kind and so happy. Surely they would have been married.

But back to Malcolm. After that car accident he spent two weeks in the hospital and then he called his father. Otto bought him a plane ticket home and he never left again. He took over the store in town; I'm sure you've seen him there. He's had a few girlfriends along the way but if he ever did fall in love again he never told me as much. I do know that he drinks; I can smell it on his breath and I see the bottles in the shop and besides that I suppose a mother might just be able to tell that sort of thing. He wanders around town, too. When he's done with work he just wanders the way he did when he was a boy. I know he is a good person but he is not a satisfied or a brave person and often I find myself wondering where it is we went wrong.

Oh, but I don't fool myself.

I used to believe in heaven, and then I believed in *something*, and now I'm afraid all the belief has vanished from my being.

I have tried to be simple and kind in my life, and tried to do as my husband asks of me, but I have always known that my mind is quite different from his. The story of my own mother, for example—my Otto never liked that story and he forbade me to tell it as though it were true. But it is the truth, Alice, at least it certainly is to me. And what else do we have in this life? My mother was named Ida and she followed a call that led her out upon the frozen lake and by that lake she was swallowed. Those tall rocks that stand in our lake today rose up immediately after she fell within. Year after year I have looked to those rocks waiting for some apparition to come forth, to no avail.

What a crazy old woman I make myself sound!

Perhaps I mean only to say that devoid of belief as I may be, I do still know that the world is more mysterious and grand than we could ever conceive of, and that I am ever so sorry that we gave you up.

To hear Signe tell it, she and I were the only relations of Eleonora's to be spared by the lake. In it all other ancestors perished. Over the years, I often wondered if perhaps the lake had placed a curse over us. But how could that be so?

Shame. For shame we gave you up. Otto was too ashamed that his son had had a love affair, especially one with a girl beneath his class. Yet my shame was just as great: to speak against my husband, to let the curtain fall and have all the viewers see that we up on the hill were not a happy couple. So I remained utterly polite.

I don't want to leave this earth with regrets, Alice, but it looks as though I may have to. I have written hundreds of letters to you but still have not had the courage to send even one. Did you ever stay up nights wondering who you were? I am at the stage now where to die would not be a sadness but a welcome change. I want to hang on only to care for Otto. But when he is gone, I hope only that I can return to the lake, to our flawed and immutable family.

# The Old Factory

## 1982

THE RIVER LUMBERS through town, and if you walk the old rail-road track across the river and then up the bald hill, you come to a brick building that most people in town believe to have been a factory.

But why would the factory be up on the hill and not down by the river?

No matter, the librarian knew the true history of the building, and she kept an ancient newspaper cutout about it in her drawer at the circulation desk, but in all her years at that library no one ever asked her about the building, so she had never said. The old factory, everyone called it.

Redbrick, boarded-up windows, tired grass and dirt surrounding. In at least the last twenty years, no one who went there had ever seen anyone else there. That's part of why young Gerald Hughes Junior agreed to go there with his little sister, Rose; he wouldn't be seen. Also because he didn't have friends and when they got home from school that day their mother told them that their father had the day off and that they were to skedaddle, their parents wanted some peace and quiet.

"Won't be quiet," Gerald said, and his mother went red.

It was a gray and cold day and they lived in a railcar next to their grandparents, who also lived in a railcar. The big river ran behind their houses, and tumbled right there in view to the mill dam. Their grandfather had worked in the mill but the mill had long since shut down. At their grandparents' house their grandmother wanted them to stay quiet, their grandfather was sick—he always was, he'd had to retire early for this, a cough and a stiff back and a general inability to rise from bed—and today he had finally fallen asleep. The kids whispered for a bit with their grandmother in the small kitchen.

"Gerald," their grandmother said. "Do you know how many cookies you just ate?"

"No, ma'am," he said.

"Twenty-two, I been counting."

Gerald looked in awe at his grandmother and Rose looked with the same eyes at her own brother and then the three of them fell into laughter. From the back bedroom their grandfather grunted.

"Get," their grandmother said, and smacked their bottoms.

Rose was seven and Gerald was nine. Rose looked across the river and up the hill and the sun fell in one beam onto that old factory. It was speaking to her, calling to her, she believed that. There was something in that building that had pulled the sun to it, and something in the universe that pulled her eyes to the sun.

"Gerald," she said. "I have the most extra-ordinary feeling."

Gerald picked up a stick and a rock and hit the rock with the stick. He watched to see the rock land in the river but he did not see it.

"I've got to go to the old factory," she said.

"Okay," said Gerald.

"You've got to come with me." Not really, he didn't have to, but without him she knew she would be bored and perhaps a little afraid.

"Don't matter to me," he said, so Rose headed to the trestle. Gerald ran up behind her and grabbed her by the upper arms and gave her a little shake right there at the edge. The river was at least twelve feet below and if she fell she would surely die. She screamed and Gerald pulled her back steady and let go and ran on and she ran after him.

At the top of the hill Rose collapsed in the dirt and grass. She spread her arms and her legs out, a giant starfish, and she breathed heavily. Gerald circled around her and threw rocks at the building. The clouds moved over Rose and hit the building, and from her angle, on the ground, it was as though the building were eating the clouds.

"Wait," she said slowly. She put her fingers to her temples. "Wait, right there, hold it, Rose," she said to herself.

"Hush up," her brother said.

"Eliza Plimpton!" she said.

"Whatever."

"Eliza Plimpton, I see it all! I'm having a psychicness, Gerald! Eliza Plimpton and her sister and parents lived in the country and then her father died because a cow sat on him!"

Gerald laughed.

"A lot of people laughed but it was a truly sad event," she said, her voice now floating miles away. "Eliza Plimpton, who dreamed only of becoming a sled maker, had to come to town to work in this factory. I see it all, Gerald. She worked in this factory and she took a room at the bottom of the hill where twenty women slept in bunk beds. Each morning she walked up the hill to take her post at the factory. She has only now just come into me, Gerald." It was true. The name, though it meant nothing, had simply appeared in the girl's mind.

"Big deal," Gerald said.

"Now the great mystery is why she came to me only just here now. How many people you think worked in this factory?" The building was shading the sun, and the red bricks had become darker, like dried blood. Rose still lay on the ground, and she looked up sidelong at her brother, who, beneath that great old factory, seemed incomprehensibly small. It wasn't a look of defeat it gave him, though, but a look of wonder. With her miniature brother Rose could venture across the whole planet, all in secret. She stood up and walked to what used to be a window but was now a sun-bleached stretch of plywood. She put her small dirty fingers at the bottom edge of the plywood and it lifted right up. Dust clouds flew out to her.

Rose dropped the wood and ran to the next boarded window. It would not lift. Three more she tried and no other window would lift.

"That is something!" she yelled to her brother. "Now you tell me, why did I choose this window first?" She was back at the window that lifted. "S-I-G-N, brother man!" She ran the backside of her hand across her forehead; her endless capabilities exhausted her. When she gathered her breath and lifted the plywood and began to squeeze her body in between it and the building, her brother came and pulled her out and pushed her aside and he crawled right up, the skinny little thing, and lifted himself through the window. He called to his sister from inside and she lifted the plywood once more and he grabbed her wrists and pulled and in she came.

Brick, dust, streaks of light like the wings of a god or some great being. Silence in the building and in the children's hearts, too. Rose's hand went out and grabbed her brother's and he didn't squeeze back but he didn't pull away, either. They were in the dark and pink stomach of a giant. Above them what used to be a ceiling had turned to a maze of beams and light and darkness. Dust in Rose's mouth, and her brother's. The floor dust only, whatever it had been before gone now. And the smell, not like an old book and not like an old house but something in between. Not that machine smell that you might expect from a factory. Rose breathed it in and closed her eyes and watched as this woman, Eliza Plimpton, laid herself down in her bottom bunk and pulled a starched white sheet up to her neck. The sheet perfectly creased over the top of the blanket, a little white lip to hold her in. Rose watched as in the dark purple morning Eliza Plimpton walked up the great hill on what used to be a dirt road but now was grown over. Workers behind her and workers in front of her, all along the hill. Hundreds of lunch pails in hundreds of hands. What were they going to make?

"Buttons," Rose said, and picked up a red button from the dirt floor. It was the first word that either of them spoke inside the building, and just after the word dropped so, too, did something across the way. It wasn't a crash or a scurry but just a movement, like a clearing of the throat, a movement to announce a presence. When Rose and Gerald looked from the button to the direction of the noise it was through large shafts of light that moved in singular strands like the shadows of long, flying people.

Rose moved across the building first. Her brother wouldn't have done it. But since she did he had to follow.

"Hello?" she called. "Olly olly oxen free." A bird soared down from a rafter and then up in small circles. "This ain't no place to live," Rose said.

Toward the middle of the building the disparate strands of

light found a home together, and from there they stretched eastward in one great path. That path ended in the corner. There was nothing in the building—at least not on this floor—no old tables or chairs, no machines. But over in the corner where the light fell there was a shoebox. Rose approached it gently, as though it were a new friend who might be scared off. She touched it. Warm from the sun. She sat down and her brother stood over her and when she opened the old blue box and removed a folded piece of paper and read, "Dear Simon," her brother grabbed the letter and the box from her.

"True love!" Rose exclaimed. "Eliza Plimpton found her true love!"

The paper had an extra crinkle to it, as if it had been wet and then dried. Yellow legal paper, a kind neither Gerald nor his sister had ever written upon before. Gerald read the letter to himself. *Dear Simon, The lake calls out to me. Sometimes I dream of walking into it and resuming life beneath. I read once of the spirits of the water, how they do in fact call to people, sometimes with benevolence* (Gerald did not understand that word, not the sound or the sense of it) *and sometimes harm in mind. I listen to the loons and am sure their call is one of pure love. When will you come to the island, Simon?*

"Puke," Gerald said. He put the letter back in the box where there were at least twenty more with it and put the box under his arm and told his sister to follow; they were leaving the old factory.


That night Rose and Gerald had dinner with their grandparents, and after dinner Rose took the box from under her chair (she'd kept it there while they ate) and got her flashlight from beneath the couch cushion and put her coat on and went out to keep her nightly watch for Tasha, who had just moved to the neighbor-hood. Tasha walked by each night on her way home from work at the nursing home, and to Rose, she was the most kind and beautiful woman to ever be put upon the earth.

Outside, Rose felt she could hear the coldness of the river. The leaves were just beginning to drop so as Rose sat there under the sugar maple with her box of letters and a flashlight, every once in a while a leaf would flutter down before her, and it seemed to her to be endlessly romantic. There were words in these letters that she didn't understand, but there was one word that the girl's letters always had: love. *How I love the look of the lake at night. This island fills me with pure love. Love, Alice.* The man's letters weren't so romantic, but they were there, a response to each letter Alice had sent. His letters said "lonely" a lot of the time—*Work all day and my dog gets lonely. Lonely up north where I'm working now. You out on the island all alone must be lonely.* Also his letters had one sentence nearly every time, *Be on the island soon.* And once: *Ninety-nine percent sure I'm in love with you. The one percent left is waiting to talk to your eyes.*

Oh! Rose read that and fell right over into the cold grass and leaves.

"What you got?" Tasha asked, when she appeared. (And how Tasha would have liked to see those letters. Of course she didn't know that it was her Kenneth who had stolen them, but had she seen the letters she would have figured it out.)

At first, for about a week, Rose had only said hello to Tash, and then after nearly two weeks she had gathered the courage to go out to the sidewalk and introduce herself. Now it had been nearly two months and Rose knew things about Tasha that nearly no one else in the world knew, like that Tasha had left her love, Kenneth, and lived alone now. She knew that at night Tasha's greatest joy was to fix herself a plate of food and then do all the dishes and wipe all the counters before sitting down to eat. She'd have to heat the meal up again, but when she sat down to eat the entire house sparkled around her, silent and still. Also she knew that Tash had left her dogs with Kenneth when she left him, so now no one in the world needed a single thing from her, except when she was at work.

Rose stuffed the letters back into the box and put it behind her back. "How's Mrs. Lewis?"

"Same," Tash said. "Only today she thinks it was me and not her son bought her the new pillow."

"And Sophie? Did she come today?"

"Don't you have a good memory," Tash said. She told the girl that dear Sophie Wickholm—who was in her seventies but still put her shoes on and marched herself all the way down the hill and over to the nursing home each Wednesday morning to play the piano for the residents—had indeed come today.

"It's good to have a friend you can talk to," Rose said to Tasha, because Tasha had told her that though Sophie was an old woman, the two had become the sort of friends who could say nearly anything to each other. Rose wanted that sort of friend.


Lately Rose had been having a problem sleeping, though her family didn't know it. Most of the time she could fall asleep when she lay down, but by the time the moon was up over her house she'd be awake again. For a few weeks she'd just lain there in her bed staring at the wall and trying to stay perfectly still, but finally she'd tired of that and crept outside. There she would just stand in the yard and look up at the sky and open her arms and breathe and feel filled up and nearly free. One night when a car drove by and honked Rose lifted her fist and yelled at the driver to stop interrupting her peace and quiet. She bit down on her lip and kicked the tree and then she said, "Damn it all, Justin Green."

That was it, it was out. She'd looked around to make sure

no one had heard her. She hadn't said his name since the day it had happened. But after it was out there, floating in the air, Rose crept back in and found her flashlight and walked down the road to his house and there she stared up at his window and held a rock in her hand, but she hadn't thrown it that night or any night since.

Tonight Rose put the box of letters under the covers, at the base of her bed, and kept her feet touching them as she drifted off to sleep.

"Oh, it's heaven," she said aloud. She meant it was heaven to be Alice and in love.


It took a week for Rose to get to the bottom of the pile of letters and realize that there was a problem. That they went back and forth, Alice Thorton at 33 Bear Island, Kettleborough, and Simon Wentworth at PO Box 59, Kettleborough, but that toward the end of each one of them Alice kept saying she wished she would hear from Simon, and Simon kept saying he wished he would hear from Alice. And then those last few letters: *I suppose you don't love me.* Or, *I shall interpret your silence as a wish to remain alone.* It was when Rose woke up in the night to a wind so heavy her window rattled that it suddenly came to her, she had her hands on long-lost love letters, and that somewhere in the world there floated two loveless people who were in fact in love.

"Oh my God!" Rose yelled. When her grandmother awoke to the sound and came rushing into the room—for on some nights Rose liked to sleep at her grandparents' house, in her grandfather's nightshirt—Rose told her it was a ghost, that she had seen the ghost of Eliza Plimpton. What else could she say? Her grandmother in that tattered white nightgown, it was the first image to come to Rose's mind.

"Get yourself to sleep, you fool," her grandmother said.

That morning at breakfast Rose wouldn't eat.

"You sick, honey?"

"I done picked myself up a broken heart," Rose told her.

Rose's brother had lost interest in the letters, and Rose hadn't told her grandmother about them, so she knew she was basically doomed to suffer alone. No one had yet taught her how to use a telephone book to look up the writers, and besides that, Rose was nearly certain that these letters were ancient, and all that would be left of the lovers was their lonely ghosts. She didn't know that the dates were right there on the envelopes—that these letters had ended not two months ago. She pushed her bowl of cereal to the middle of the table and dropped her head onto her arms.

"Oh, all the world for Alice Thorton and Simon Wentworth," she said.

Her grandmother was at the sink, listening to the radio, and when she heard that she just let go of the glass in her hand and it shattered. She left the pieces there and went to her granddaughter and tilted the girl's chin her way and she said, "What? What is it you've gotten yourself into?"

"A twisted love affair of a time gone by!" Rose cried out.

"Those names, what did you say? Tell me those names again."

Rose looked at her grandmother and in her eyes there was a look she never had seen before. The darks of her eyes were fluttering right there in the center of the white.

"Alicia Thermos and Silo Wentaway," Rose said quickly.

"Say it again."

"Alison Thermin and Simone Wendell!" Her chin was in her grandmother's hand and Rose herself was sweating.

"That's not what you said."

"I made it up, I made it up, I got myself an imaginating mind!"

Pam let go of her granddaughter. Anyway, she had been listening to that old song. She might have misheard the girl after all. "Get," she said. "Go get yourself to school."

Rose went to the bedroom and put the letters in the bottom of her schoolbag and went out to meet her brother on the curb. Which meant that behind her Rose had left no trace; that though her grandmother scoured her own house and Rose's parents' house, too, she found not one sign of Alice Thorton.

"I thought I heard something today," Pam said to her dear friend Valerie Hill. They were at Valerie's place, a big old house that her silence had bought her. Back when Valerie had still been drinking was the last time the two of them had ever talked about it, or the girl. Back then, when letters postmarked in Oregon came from Jennifer to Malcolm, at least those rich Wickholms had flown Valerie out across the country and put her up in a hotel to search for her missing daughter. But—and only Pam knew this—by the time Valerie returned, alone, her empty house had been paid off and the infant—her own grandbaby—announced in the paper as Alice Thorton. Amid the haze that followed was the only time Pam had ever heard Valerie question the events. Had Valerie's Jennifer and Karl Wickholm planned to leave their infant like that? Valerie couldn't believe that her Jennifer, sixteen years old and still dressing her dolls, would have deserted her own infant at the edge of the lake. But what about Karl? Was his car accident a mistake? Had Jennifer been in that crash that killed him? Is that why she ran? Had they abandoned the baby first? Our Karl, those Wickholms had said. Our Karl cannot date a Hill.

Pam lifted the tea bag out of her mug and wrapped the string tightly around the leaves until all the liquid was squeezed out. She carried it to the trashcan with one hand held beneath it in case it dripped. She pressed her foot on the base of the can to lift its top and as it opened she said quickly, "Alice Thorton. Thought I heard my Rose say that."

"Well," Valerie said. "I got to get myself going on my errands."

The letters in Rose's backpack made her feel as if she had a secret strength. When she had to read aloud to the class her voice did not tremble. When she went to the chalkboard to subtract a three-digit number from a four-digit number, she got it right even though she had to stand there in front of everyone, Justin Green included, while she counted backward with her fingers. It was at recess that the problem started.

"Why you got to bring your backpack out with you?"

"Hush up," Rose said.

"No one else brings a bag out."

Rose shrugged and pulled at a clump of her own hair, then put it right in her mouth and chewed.

"Gross as I always thought you was." This was Justin Green. His first words to her since that day.

"Open your bag and show us what you got," he said.

Rose spit the hair from her mouth, and the wet clump of it stuck there against her cheek. The fence that went around the school playground had one opening in it, there at the back by the willow tree. She could crawl through that and go home. The day was gray and it made the whole world look dirty. She crossed her arms in front of her chest and she said, "Maybe I got a secret mission in this world."

"Maybe you got yourself girl troubles," he said. "Because you're disgusting like I always thought."

The others heard that, and when the bell rang and they all went in no one would walk next to Rose, believing that she

indeed had girl troubles—something they only vaguely understood but certainly thought of as dirty. Rose kept her bag in
her lap and throughout the rest of the day she prayed silently
to Alice Thorton and Simon Wentworth to save her from her
misery.

The worst part was when the trains went by. The rumble made
the floor of the school vibrate in a way Rose had never realized
before. It sent that same looseness to her teeth that she'd felt out
there on the track in the summer with Justin Green. What they'd
done out there felt nothing like what Alice Thorton would ever
feel with Simon Wentworth. The thought of it made her stomach hurt. And then after, the way he'd held her down with his
teeth clenched and her shoulders on the iron track. A train had
been coming, getting closer all the time, and he wouldn't let her
up and he just kept saying it, *You're disgusting, you're disgusting
and now I'm going to make you die.* The taste of his tongue had still
been in her mouth and Rose had spit it in his face, she hadn't
been afraid.


Rose's brother walked home ahead of her, he always did, so Rose
was alone and speaking a little to herself as she walked. Alice
Thorton, she was saying, I understand the longing that you feel,
left foot, right foot, don't step on a crack, I, too, long for the lake
and to feel at home with another human being. She didn't know
she was being followed, and when she felt a tug at her backpack
she thought a strap had let loose so she stopped, and before she
had turned around Justin Green had thrown her into the bush
at the side of the road, which was alongside a steep hill. Dirt in
Rose's hair, her backpack crushed in the dirt beneath her.

"What is it?" he demanded. "What's so secret?"

Rose kicked but she did not scream; she didn't want any single person to find her here in the bushes with Justin Green. He pulled her hair and turned her over, gritting his teeth all the while, and he dug her face into the dirt. Months ago, after Justin Green stopped being her friend and became the worst person in the world, Rose had borrowed her brother's jackknife and with it sharpened the tip of a piece of wood. She had planned to use it for protection—she had had the sense that she would need to and now she knew she had been right. Rose pulled that piece of wood out of her pocket and she jammed it into Justin Green's body as hard as she could. In it went, right into his stomach. He screamed and whimpered and Rose Hughes picked up her backpack and ran down the street without looking back.

One night, long ago, Rose had sat with her brother at the top of the hill by the factory, looking down on sleeping Kettleborough. That time, Rose had looked at the houses and received from them the distinct feeling that she could understand the lives of the people inside. Like the world and all the people within it made sense to her. Now when she looked down on that small place and the dark lake that rose up behind it, Rose bit her lip harder and pulled at her hair and then released and began to pound her open hands against the sides of her head. Love didn't exist, not anything like it. Goodness neither. Rose had killed— she believed she had—and now she and all the world were doomed.

Now to the factory Rose had brought matches, a blanket, and a jackknife, which she borrowed from her grandfather's top drawer. Food she had not bothered with because she had not been sure how long she intended to survive. Water, though— she had taken an empty milk jug from the trashcan and filled it in the sink. The letters, too, of course she had those. And a flashlight. Darkness fell early and when it did Rose was already in the corner of the factory, a blanket wrapped around her. She bit her lip until it bled. She shook, too, from fear or cold or both. When she heard a creak she held her breath and imagined that a criminal had been lurking in the woods, waiting for her, had watched her enter the building. She imagined him now coming upon her and stabbing her to death. As she had done to Justin Green. Rose held the jackknife open, tight in her fist. In this way she passed what felt like half the night, though in truth it was scarcely an hour. By eight o'clock the moon had risen over the crest of the hill, and it was near full, and it sent light into the building—enough to illuminate the quick swoop and dart of hundreds of bats. No more could she bear it. Rose gathered her things and crawled across the floor, back to the boarded window she had entered through.

When she lit the fire, it was after she had worn herself out with tears and cold and with the work of gathering sticks and carrying them back up the hill. In that terrible night the moon had spread a light upon the hill that looked beautiful—there was that, Rose had the sense to recognize it. As she walked back and forth up the hill and down she imagined herself as a girl sitting upon the moon and watching this Rose toil. She would remember that—that image of herself as a small being working dutifully upon the land.

It had only been to warm herself, but then she had opened her backpack and thrown those letters in and watched them burn one by one. Ain't no love exists in the world, she had said to herself. When she threw the last letter in Rose lay back and looked up at the moon. The grass was high, there had been no rain for weeks, and she understood this. She had made a fire ring of rocks. And she had the milk jug of water there, which she intended, once she sat up, to pour over the flames.

"Go out there," Gerald's grandmother told him. "Just go up and down the street and call her name." When he'd begun to put on his boots she'd said, "That Tasha. Go down the street and see if Rose isn't with her."

Gerald began to call her name before he was even outside. He wasn't worried, Rose often disappeared, but it felt good to yell anyway. He picked up a stick and a rock and as he yelled her name he nailed the rock with the stick and looked up in the moonlight to see where the rock flew and when he did he saw that hillside lit up like a forest of sunflowers in full bloom.

By the time Gerald and his family got to the edge of the fire, no one had yet found the little girl. The fire department was already there, along with nearly the whole of Kettleborough. Kenneth was there, and Simon, too. In silence the two watched the flames, and something about the hillside burning gave Kenneth the sense that it was time, that this little life would not last forever and that he ought to confess his sin of being a criminal of a postman by stealing all of those letters. The heat from the flames made him sweat and he unzipped his jacket and looked around. Across the way he saw his Tash, standing in close to Sophie Wickholm.

"Well," Kenneth said to Simon. He meant to go on, to say that he himself had broken the law, that Alice had loved Simon and that he had the proof, he'd hidden it right there not twenty yards away, just there in the northwest corner of the factory where he and Tash used to go with blankets and candles when they were teenagers and in love. He cleared his throat and looked once more at Tasha, lit up by the light of the flames, and she looked at him, too, and he knew then that she was remembering the very same thing. "Simon," Kenneth said, but just then the firemen pushed through, splitting Simon and Kenneth apart from each other, carrying that little girl.

Up on the hill, with Kettleborough residents together in the glow of the fire, Simon scanned the crowd for the woman he imagined to be Alice. Patty Jean out on the island had told him she had moved to town. "Love letters?" Patty Jean had said. "You never once met the girl?" She had laughed and Simon had smiled as though he, too, was entertained by the notion, but in truth the fact of it kept him up through the night with no one but his own dog to talk to. A hundred times he could have met her but instead he had chosen to be a coward. Now he believed that by love he would know her when he saw her. Everybody was here—why wouldn't she be? He would be brave. Like a crazed man he pushed through that crowd, searching.

Sophie could have told him that the girl whose face shone so clearly of her own dead Karl's was not up there on the hill. Malcolm, too, for though he was drunk and though he was silent he certainly had the clarity to know his own brother's daughter when he saw her. And in fact he had seen her—tonight when Malcolm left his shop downtown and headed up the hill he'd seen that girl whom in those weeks after his brother had died he had held and rocked and loved so dearly. Grown now, she had been standing on the pier, watching the lake so intently that she had not even noticed the fire, lit by her own love letters, that raged on the hill behind her, or the sirens that passed by, rushing that burned little girl to the doctor.

.   .   .

But Rose would heal. In the hospital she would learn that Justin Green had required stitches but had lived, and that she herself had been cursed with a scar that ran from the tip of her toe up the entire surface of her leg and then stretched like the branch of a maple across her midsection, with one limb extending up her neck and brushing against her ear. That seemed all right to her. With her scar as remembrance of the pain she had caused, it seemed to Rose that the world and all that was in it might perhaps contain a trace—and only a trace—of order.

# Return

## 1982

WHEN I CAME off the island, I was lucky to find this small house to rent, and luckier still to find that the store needed a baker. Now, while the rest of Kettleborough sleeps, I plunge my hands into living, breathing yeast. The solitude of it suits me; my days on the island prepared me for such a quiet life. I enter the store around midnight, and it doesn't open until six a.m. By seven I am on my way home to sleep. When I wake, in the afternoon, I walk through town and the woods, and often I find myself in the old cemetery at the end of Main Street. The stones there are the oldest I have ever seen. Many are small and thin, some have crumbled right apart under the weight of the years, and others have long ago lost their names and dates. The ones that lie flat in the ground are the ones I like the best. Moss and grass push up around their edges, reminding me that the earth is slowly taking them in.

A line of old maple trees forms a perfect square around the cemetery, and when the trees are heavy with leaves it makes that small place seem like a room cut off from the rest of the world. When the leaves drop, the stone wall that runs just in front of the trees becomes more visible, so even without the leaves the cemetery remains set off from the land around it, and to stand outside the wall is quite a different experience than to stand within it. This year, as the leaves dropped, I took care to keep them off the graves. Once, after I discovered his name, I read all the stones, looking for it, Karl Wickholm, but it's not there.

On one of these evenings in the cemetery, when the leaves had just fallen and the bare maple arms cast shadows that made it seem that I was in the palm of a great and glowing hand, a skinny little girl came in repeating a name.

"Eliza Plimpton, Eliza Plimpton!" she said breathlessly.

"Here," I told her, for though that name meant nothing to me, I had seen the grave, and I led her to it.

That girl was astonished; she put her hand to her head and let her jaw drop and after a moment she looked slowly around the cemetery and then she held out her hand and asked me to pinch her, which I did, gently, and she said, "So it's true, this is real life?"

I assured her it was. She told me that some weeks ago the name had come to her, dropped down into her mind like a ray of light, and since that time she had been certain—though her brother mocked her—that this woman surely had existed. She ran her hands over the gravestone. I told her about tracing graves with a sheet of paper and a pencil, which she said she would certainly do. I went right along with her; I acted as though I, too, was astonished that the name had come to her and had turned out to be a real name of a real Kettleborough woman. In truth I suspected that she had heard this name before, in school or in the walls of her own house, where it could be that this very woman had lived, or on a field trip to one of the old mills around, or maybe even in the cemetery itself. But like I said, I went along with the girl, amazed at the sheer magic of it.

It wasn't until a few weeks after the fire on the hillside that I saw that little girl again. I entered the cemetery and there she lay, so still, her head resting upon Eliza Plimpton's grave. Because of the dried leaves my entrance made noise, but the girl did not even look up. I went to her and said something, I don't remember what—"Excuse me?" or "Are you all right?"—and she didn't respond. Finally I reached out and touched her upon the head. At this point she let out the sigh of an adult upon whose shoulders an incomprehensible weight has been placed.

"All the world," she said heavily. She was utterly worn out.

By this time I had kneeled down beside her. When I asked her what the trouble was she finally looked up, surprised, I think, that anyone should bother to ask. And there was her face; I knew it right away. She had been in the papers—the little girl who had started the fire. Rose Hughes, and now with those wide and glistening eyes I saw that my old friend Gerald Hughes was indeed her father, and I was astonished that I had not realized that the first time I met her. Still, I pretended I had heard nothing of the fire, and instead asked her once more what the trouble was.

She moved from the grave and lay down in the leaves, her arms spread out wide. Here she breathed loudly for a few minutes, and then she lifted her shirt and showed me her scar—I had heard she had scarred severely—and she said, "I have my mark. The world is a fair place."

"I don't know about that," I said.

Rose lifted her legs straight up and then let them drop to the ground.

"I have ruined the only true love I ever knew," she told me.

"You were in love?" I asked her.

"Oh," she said. "Oh, to be in love."

"I know," I told her.

Just then the church bell rang; it was five o'clock. Rose jumped up and ran out of the cemetery.


In the afternoons I also spend hours at the library. There's a wonderful old woman there who worked for years as the head librarian but retired at least two decades ago. She's ninety-seven now. "All my friends are dead," she says frequently. Her husband, too, and though she has children, "good ones," they have gone off to live their own lives. Now she spends her days as I imagine she did when she worked, and by now she must have read every book in that library. She's still sharp, too—in fact, I took her mind for granted when I first met her. For she says things—on that first day I met her she said, "I should think you would come around," and then on another day, "Don't you look like your grandmother." Shamefully, I took these things for the remarks of an old woman who had gotten confused.

On that first visit to the library, I told the old librarian that I wanted to find out about the history of the lake. She gave me a pile of ancient, fragile books. Their covers were cloth or leather, black or green or dark blue, and their pages had yellowed to the color of firewood. There were books about the boats of the lake; books about the islands and the Indians who first settled them; books that describe the geology in a grand, celebratory way; and there was one book that documented the legends people have told of the lake. Typically, these books were not allowed to be taken out of the library, but the old librarian slipped each one into a plastic cover and sent me home with them, saying I had two weeks. In just three days I had already been through all of them, but I kept them for the allotted time. They revealed nothing for me, but with them in my hands I had the strange feeling that some part of myself had been described.

When, after two weeks, I replaced the books in their plastic covers and walked them back to the library, the old librarian put her hand on mine and said, "You just take them out any old time." After that she led me to the microfiche, where she taught me how to flip through old editions of the *Kettleborough News*. "When were you born?" she asked me, and suggested I start looking there, and in the days and weeks that surrounded that day.

At that point, I had not yet told her that I was truly on a search for my own history. Yet as I looked through the papers that she had led me to, almost immediately I came upon a name I had wanted to find: Wickholm. This was Karl Wickholm. His crashed Ford was pictured right there on the front page of the evening paper. I can only hope their family was spared that evening's edition. It wasn't too many issues later until I discovered myself, announced as the new child of Clara and Paul Thorton.

When I left the library that day, the librarian didn't say a word. She just put her hand on my shoulder and walked me to the door, and even opened the door for me. The sun was bright, blinding, and it was clear to me that though I was still unsure about just where I had come from, she certainly knew. Now, as I walk through this town, I wonder just how many people know my story, and how it is possible that in all these years, no one has ever thought to tell it to me.

·　　·　　·

It was around this time that a woman appeared at the back counter of the store and rang that bell one solid time. I had never heard anyone ring it before, for usually I am gone before the first customer arrives. I was startled when I heard it ring, and jumped. I came out to the counter in my white coat and hat and immediately I recognized her. I had not seen her in years, but I would have known her anywhere—the woman who would stand outside the school fence while we children played hopscotch or four-square at recess. Then, as now, she wore a fitted skirt and suit jacket, held her hands clasped neatly at her waist, and did not let one piece of her tightly permed hair ever fall out of place. Of course I always assumed that she was someone else's grandmother.

Over the years, I saw her on the pier, too, looking toward Bear Island with that same urgency that I have learned to look toward that place with. Once, when I was a child, I saw her at a ski race of mine. And what about the day when I was fourteen years old, running home from the Hughes's railcar after I had been scolded and mocked? I was so depleted on that day, and when I tripped on the sidewalk and landed on my hands and knees, her small feet were there in front of me. I remember noticing that her laces were tied so neatly, each loop the same size as the other, and all of it centered perfectly on her stiff shoes. She kneeled down and helped me up, and took my hands into her soft ones. The time she dared, I can now say. She looked into my eyes and said without doubt, "You are accepted."

These days, I find myself wondering if she could have known, back then, that those words would mean something to me. Her gentle blue eyes, her soft hands—I believed that she held some grace far beyond this world that allowed her to see right into me. How very different those words would have been had I known they came from a grandmother who had failed to take me in.

"Alice," she said as she stood at the counter.

"Yes?"

"Sophie Wickholm," she said, and held out her hand.

I have Hill hands. When I was young and paired with Martha Hill for a school project, I noticed, all those years before she became my dear friend, that she and I had the same awkwardly angled pointer fingers that push inward, toward the next finger in line. The same long, straight thumbs, too, and the same blunt nails that will never be shaped into something delicate and beautiful, as Sophie's are.

I took her hand, shook, and returned to my work.


On the night that the hillside burned, I heard the call of a loon. The water was so cold, and that poor creature should have long since fled for the south. When the call would not quit I ducked beneath the pier's railing and there I found an old canoe tied to a solitary pine tree at shore. I untied the boat and climbed in and paddled until I was an equal distance from mainland and Bear Island. It was not something I had ever done before, and it was not my boat, but the night was so lovely, and I wanted to be nearer to that loon. When I looked back toward home, I saw its hill flicker and shine. It took me a moment to realize it was burning. *Go to sleep,* I bade the loon, who called so urgently, as though she believed it was her job to save Kettleborough. Yet she would not quit; her call rang out until the fire calmed, so together for hours we floated as the ash of our town drifted down upon us like snow.

I told the old librarian about that. She wears bright, colorful clothes such as I have never seen in Kettleborough, and she speaks so unabashedly about my life. "You're a strange one," she likes to say to me, and "Get married and have your babies fast." I'm not sure if she was always this way, or if her boldness has come with age, but either way it is an inspiration for me. "Why are you shy?" she demands. When I told her about the loon she took my hands in her soft, trembling ones. "You be careful with that call," she said.

Her warning was so serious, so firm, but this only made me curious, so as the weather grew colder I listened more intently. Twice I believed I heard it. I was at work each time, and immediately I lifted my hands from the dough and ran to the front of the store and pushed the door open with my hip, my hands dripping with water and flour, and crossed the street to the pier. By then the call was gone, and I doubted that I had ever heard it.

And then one time, in the cemetery, I was sure I heard it, but I did not chase it. That was when Rose reappeared.

"I'm Alice," I told her, and she swooned, she actually did; she put her arm to her forehead and she tipped back and exhaled, and then the little girl tipped right over.

"Rose!" I called, and kneeled down at her side. I tapped her cheeks and said her name again.

"Pinch me," she said, so I did, gently, for the second time. Again she asked me whether or not this was real, true life, and again I told her it was.

"So you're psychic?" she asked.

"No," I said. "Are you?"

With the palm of her hand she hit herself in the head; she was demonstrating her stupidity, trying to say that of course she held no such power. I reached out for her and helped her up, and she stood for just one moment and then sat back down, her legs crossed, and she asked me to sit with her. She wanted to know if she could trust me, and I assured her she could, and then she spit into the palm of her hand and held it out. I shrugged and did the same; already I loved this wild girl. We shook.

"Now tell me one of your secrets or fears." This, she said,

would seal our handshake. I already knew she dreamed of love so I told her that I had fallen in love out on an island, but that the man had not loved me back.

"Simon!" Rose shouted.

"Yes," I said, taken aback.

Immediately she began to quote the letters that I had sent to Simon, and others that she said he had meant to send to me. She told me she had found them, she told me she had burned them, and then she lay back and spread her arms and threw dead leaves up so they would fall down upon her and she kicked her legs and she yelled, "All the world for Alice Thorton and Simon Wentworth!"

She wanted to know where I lived. She said she would find Simon; she would enlist her best friend, Tasha Stevenson, as she had known she should have done weeks ago. I said that she was to do no such thing. For only now had I begun to pull myself back up from the depths, steady and alone. I told her I did not want to meet him. Yet I knew my pleas would be meaningless, for here was a child who had done wrong, and now here was a great world offering up a chance for her to mend what she had broken. I have never been offered such a chance, and I was not going to steal this one from a girl who so desperately wanted to believe in the order and fairness of creation.

Just three days later Rose had succeeded in her plan; I looked out the window to see that small girl tugging a man at least four times her size up the walkway to my door. When she had arranged him at the front door she knocked and then tucked herself behind his body.

I opened the door and he said my name. I could see his shirt tighten; Rose was pulling at it from behind. I told her to go along and immediately she did, winking suggestively as she left, walking backward and stumbling on her own feet. When she was gone I welcomed Simon in. It was a strange occasion but by then we both understood how fleeting and breakable our love could be; we understood to take care. I asked him if he might like to go for a walk. He spoke of his work and I spoke of mine, we spoke of Kettleborough, and finally we came around to the lake. He said his father had died when he was a boy, and that though his mother had taken care of him she had not made the time for him, not really, and this had left him with days upon days of nothing to do but go out on the water. That's how he met Malcolm—as a boy he'd had some trouble with a boat and Malcolm had helped him out with it, and after that had given him a job at the ice cream shop. Malcolm, Simon said, had become something like a father to him.

By then I knew the name, Malcolm Wickholm, and was fairly certain he would be my uncle, but I said nothing of it, not yet. Instead I talked of how I missed the days on the island, and how it would be a dream if one day we actually did winter out there. This made Simon shine. Hours later, when we arrived back at my door, I invited him in. We drank wine and ate bread and we did not tire of each other's company, not then or any moment since. Rose wants desperately to know when we will marry, but I will not cast out such a dream future, not to her or Simon or even to myself. For such loneliness I had known, such heartbreak, and then finally my quiet solitude worked its way in with warm bread and a library, an old, peaceful cemetery and nights alone in Kettleborough. Now here this love stands with me, breathless and awake, to fill me up. I will not say what is to become of us. But it would be a lie to say I do not want it, will not take it.

.  .  .

I don't hold it against Simon, the fact that he knew, all that time, where it was I had come from. He is not the sort to offer information that is not asked for, and though he knows I love him, he believes he ought not to walk uninvited into my private affairs. So he was delicate and uninformative the first time that I brought up the subject. About a week later, after I had gone to the courthouse and looked at documents that merely said that I had been adopted, but did not say who it was who gave me up, I was exhausted of the search and I told Simon so.

"I wish someone would just tell me," I said to him.

"Okay," Simon said.

"Sorry?"

"I can tell you if you want me to," he said.

"You can't."

"I can," he said. "I suspect that librarian of yours can tell you, too." He had picked up a fork from the table and now he tapped it nervously against his leg.

"I suppose anyone in this town can tell me," I said viciously.

"No," he said.

"But you can." He did not answer, so I went on. "And my librarian." I was humiliated.

"Only reason I know is Malcolm," he said.

"And the others?"

He shrugged.

"How many people know? Does everyone in this town know? Is that what people talk about as I walk by?"

"No," he said. He had begun to tap the fork against the table instead of his leg. It was late afternoon, the sun had already set, and outside the trees looked like dark shadows of themselves. Simon stood up and without a word walked out my door. I stood there terrified, shocked that I should make this kind man leave me. I considered chasing him out but a minute later he returned with an arm's load of wood. He opened the woodstove and I saw that the fire had gone out. As he began to poke at the coals I sat down at the table and then I stood and put a kettle on for tea, and then I sat back down again, and finally I told him to please go ahead and tell me what he knew.

. Now, there is a way that I can let the fact that I was found at the shore of the water comfort me. I can let myself believe that not only was I deposited on the lake but I was also born there, which means that sometimes, on dark or rainy days, when the sky and the lake seem to grow forth from each other with no line to say where one ends and the other begins, I can see myself as a child of that water, and not the unwanted infant that I truly was.

So I already knew by the time Sophie mustered the courage to slip the letter under my door. Though she had delivered it a week earlier, it was Christmas Eve when I finally found the strength to open the envelope and read what she had written. My father was due over for dinner, and I had a fish pie in the oven. It would be only the two of us, and neither of us would have a word to say. But so it had been for a lifetime, and though we could not speak easily, the only constant we had ever known was each other. Yet this night would be different, for I intended to tell my father all I knew.

With Sophie's letter in my hands, I suddenly smelled smoke. I checked the woodstove in the kitchen to be sure its door was properly latched. After that I went outside to see that smoke flowed unhindered from the chimney. When I returned inside the smell was gone and I thought I must have imagined it. I checked the pie in the oven—it still had at least an hour to go—and then I sat down in the living room chair. Simon had gone south to see family, Rose had not appeared in days, and the library was closed, so by now it had been about a week since I had spoken to anyone. I felt oddly strong and vacant, and found myself repeating my own name aloud. Next I went to the hall closet and pulled on my boots. I put on a coat, hat, scarf, and mittens as though it was a ritual, and without thought I went out.

Dusk, the sky a spread of pink. I walked to the pier and held my hands on the icy wooden banister, then tucked myself under and slid down the snow-covered steps. At shore there was a great mound of snow, but upon the open spread of ice there was only a dusting, for the harsh wind of winter had kept the snow from piling on the lake. I crawled over the bank and when I descended onto the ice it was as though I had been released.

Once I stood on the ice, I immediately saw that flicker of light at the tip of Bear Island. I had spent my life looking for it, and as a teenager I had made myself believe I had seen it. Now here I stood, a woman who knew that was no star reflected on the surface of the lake. The light was for me alone and as I stepped toward it I saw the being for the first time. I am not good with distances, I cannot say how many yards away it was, but perhaps the distance between that figure and my body was roughly two lengths of my own little house. By now the pink evening had been covered with a layer of dusk's blue. This being was a cutout of black, and it moved slowly, like a sad, heavy beast, back and forth across the ice. I removed my mittens and put my pointer fingers to the corners of my mouth and whistled, and it was then that that strange loon call split the air between us and traveled into me, a soft, lilting song. I began to trail after the hunched space of darkness.

There had been one surprise in Sophie's letter, and I thought of it out there on the ice: *You come from a long line of girls who have been left motherless, and from people who have a tendency to follow, no matter the consequence, any signal that might lead to beauty, even an ounce.* I understood those words as a warning, but I did not heed them. Instead, as I chased a shadow of a being through the night, I felt sharply that out there on the dark, frozen lake, some pure and ancient thread had woven itself through my ancestors, and finally sewn itself into me.

It was not an easy journey. Darkness fell quickly. At one point I looked back to see that Kettleborough had become a drop of light in the distance, and when I turned back toward where that figure had been, I could not find it. My heart began to pound in its cold cage and all the comfort I had known just minutes ago vanished. Never before had I felt so exquisitely alone. Suddenly I worried that the lake would open its mouth and claim me as its own. I began to run, and when I fell I believed, for a moment, that I saw a man floating there beneath the ice, a window held before him. I pounded and kicked desperately. That call, thankfully, interrupted me. I stood once more. I could see that I was headed to the island, and by the time I arrived I saw the figure once more. Up and down the shore she—as I would soon learn—walked, trailing a canoe at her side. Behind her my cabin looked so small and white in winter. I climbed over the bank of snow and went straight to it, thankful to be home. On the porch I let myself fall back in the snow, and I opened my scarf and let the breath of winter cover me. All the stars were lit now, and they lit up the lake, and that vision of the night sky across the water was so similar to what I had watched in summer that for a moment I was able to squint my eyes and see the mail boat pass by on its slow path to the docks. In seconds, I dreamed, I would put my sneakers on and run across the island and gather a letter from my dear Simon. Just then the woman in bearskin came up the bank of snow with her canoe, which reminded me that whatever world I was now in was not one I had ever before inhabited.

"I'll just make some dinner," I told her, as though that was the typical thing to do. She went to the door of my cabin and lifted the padlock and twisted the numbers into place and then with her arms spread wide she gathered great heaps of snow to clear a path to the door. She pushed that heavy door open and waited for me to go in, and then she followed.

There is a woodstove in there, thankfully there is, though the walls of the place are not insulated. Still, if you stay in close to the fire you can be warm enough.

"I'm all wet," she said as she held her hands over the stove.

I touched her then; she was real. The fur she wore was sopping.

"They're all in the Witches," she said, so I went to the map on the wall—we had lit candles by now—and held my finger to the spot where that great collection of rocks is marked.

When I turned back she had taken her bearskin off and hung it over the rafter. She wore wool beneath, and I put my hand to her shoulder and I said, "There, not so wet at all."

I set her before the fire. She seemed like a child, the way she stared into those flames with wonder. I went to the kitchen and took out cans, beans and corn and peas and cream of mushroom soup, and I poured them all into a pot. I felt wonderfully efficient, and fancied myself the nurse for some castaway. I took another pot and reached outside and swept it full of snow, which I put on the fire to melt.

There were sounds as we ate—I can hear them still. Slurps and chews, swallows, the sounds of her survival and the sounds of mine. We laid blankets down before the fire and beneath a great mound of wool we fell asleep.

I awoke when a cloud of stillness had been set down, when the stars were in their place and the wind had silenced. She was just slipping out the door. I knew where she would be headed. I pulled my boots on and I trailed behind her. I heard that loon call as I traveled, and I cupped my hands around my mouth to call back to it.

We went along the ice, and it took less time than I would have expected to reach the tip of the island. There those rocks the Witches rose up before us. Never had I entered them—never had any living person, so far as I knew—but now with her I did not fear life or death. I simply walked after her, through the edge of the rocks and into the forest that rose up in all directions around us. From the outside, those slick black rocks look like nothing more than a contained cluster. Yet from within that forest, those rocks stretch in all directions across the entirety of the earth. There is no sense of how to emerge. There is only a sense of how to go deeper, how to reach that oldest and tallest rock. I went there. The ice grew more and more thin. I knew it would. When the largest of the Witches stretched up before me I looked down to see the boys I had heard stories of, the ones whose hands are braided into each other's, whose bodies spin slowly to form a net. Into their arms I fell, into the cold water. I closed my eyes and in this dream state I knew that whoever that woman had been, she had draped her cloak of bearskin upon my slowly spinning body.

I do not know what became of me in that water. I do not know how I returned home. The fish pie was not burned and I was not wet. My father came to dinner. I did not tell him what I knew of my origins. I told him only that it was a Merry Christmas. I gave him the hat that I had knit for him and with terrific boldness I gave him a hug. He has been an imperfect and good enough father; he has stayed around; there still is time to love. We spoke of the lake in a way we probably both had longed for years to do, saying how lovely it was, how strong and impossible. After dinner I asked him if he might like to walk down to the pier, which he said he supposed he would. We stood there together and looked out. It was quiet but our awkwardness of each other was not resting upon our shoulders in the way it typically did.

And standing there silently with my father, looking out upon our frozen lake toward the island that I felt certain I had just traveled to, I understood that I could believe in the nothingness of my mother. The one who bore me, the one who took me in as her own for a short time—it didn't matter which. I could believe in the nothingness of her, and of my father, all fathers, even then of myself. I could believe that all of us, and the journey I had just taken, had never existed and would always exist.

But our lake—with it we were home. I was home. Home was this lake that stretched through us and down to the depths of the earth; it always had, and when we and all things were gone that home would still surge. This I knew. That never could I believe in the nothingness of our lake.

# Acknowledgments

I am honored to have had so much help while writing this book. Thank you to my writing friends, Beth McHugh, Debra Magpie Earling, and my brother Jon Keller, for inspiration and encouragement. Thank you to Deirdre McNamer for gracefully guiding me as I made my way through these characters. Thank you to my mother, Lucinda Hope, for steadfast support, and to my father, Richard Maxwell, for passing down a love of stories. Thank you to Lorna Wakefield for offering a name for both the town and the book. Thank you to my agent, Eleanor Jackson, for putting her faith in me, and to my editor, Jennifer Jackson, for steady encouragement and wise, insightful readings. I am ever grateful to the Possum Hoppers of New Hampshire, who always give me a place to come home to and write about. Finally, thank you to my husband, Jacob Maxwell, for always believing so fully in this book.

A NOTE ABOUT THE AUTHOR

Abi Maxwell was born and raised in the Lakes Region of New Hampshire, where she currently lives. She studied fiction writing at the University of Montana and now works as an assistant librarian at the Gilford Public Library. This is her first book.

A NOTE ON THE TYPE

This book was set in a version of Garamond. Claude Garamond (ca. 1480–1561) based his letter on the types of the
Aldine Press in Venice, but he introduced a number of
important differences, and it is to him that we owe the
letter now known as "old style."

*Typeset by Scribe, Philadelphia, Pennsylvania*

*Printed and bound by RR Donnelley, Harrisonburg, Virginia*

*Designed by Maggie Hinders*